A TALE OF THREE WOMEN

A TALE OF THREE WOMAN

A Tale of Three Women
Roy Glenn
© Copyright Roy Glenn 2012
Escapism Entertainment
Atlantic Beach, Florida

A TALE OF THREE WOMAN

Chapter One

It was a nasty afternoon. Thunder, lightening, wind, and rain dominated the sky. As a result, traffic was now getting to the point of being ridiculous.

"Ain't there another way you can go?" Rain looked at her watch. "I got someplace I gotta be."

"Sorry, lady."

"Fuck!" Rain shouted and pounded the seat next to h er. She found herself, along with Nick, Monika, Jackie Washington, and Xavier Assante, an old army buddy of Nick and Monika's, in a border town called McAllen, Texas.

McAllen is the largest city in Hidalgo County, Texas. It is located at the southern tip of Texas in an area known as the Rio Grande Valley. Its southern boundary is located about five miles from the US–Mexico border and the Mexican city of Reynosa, the Rio Grande, and about 70 miles west of South Padre Island and the Gulf of Mexico.

As Rain sat there, she thought back to how this all began. She was at Doc's with Nick, when Monika came in.

"What's up, Nick?" Monika asked and turned to Rain. "What's up, with you, sunshine?" she asked, noticing the big frown on her face. Before Monika walked up, Nick and Rain were deep into their usual conversation.

Wanda.

"What's up, Monika?" Nick asked, and Rain looked away.

"You'll never guess who I saw last night."

"Who?"

"Colonel Mathis," she said as she sat down.

Nick laughed, but it was nervous laughter. "Where did you see him?"

"He was in my living room last night when I got home."

"What did he want?"

"To offer me a job."

"What's the job?" Rain asked. No matter what type of mood she was in, Rain was always down for making money, and some action wouldn't hurt.

"He wants me to rob a bank," Monika said casually.

Rain shook her head. "Hold up. Is this Colonel Mathis some guy you two served under in the army?"

"That's right," Nick said.

Rain rolled her eyes at Nick and turned back to Monika. "And he wants you to rob a bank?"

Monika smiled. "In the name of the US Government."

"I don't get it," Rain said, and Nick was amused.

"You would be surprised at some of the shit ... dirty shit ... our government does," Monika said. "You'd be surprised at some of the dirty shit we've done in the name of our government."

"Still ... why does he want you to take a bank?"

"He believes that there is information in a safe deposit box that could be embarrassing to the government."

"So he wants you to take the bank as a cover to get what's in that box," Nick said understanding how things work, but Rain was still not getting it.

"At some point, they got involved with a former Mexican Judicial Federal Police agent name Félix Guzmán."

"Uncle Felix?"

"The same. The Colonel says once he broke with his government he founded the Guadalajara Cartel, and controlled all drug trade in Mexico and the trafficking corridors across the Mexico-US border. He is alleged to be the first Mexican drug chief to link up with Colombia's cocaine cartels."

"Wait a minute, they're the government; why not just get a warrant and subpoena the records?" Rain asked.

"Things like that have a tendency to make the news," Monika said. "If we do it, there is nothing to tie it to them."

"You gonna do it?" Nick asked.

"Money is right, so I'm putting a team together."

"Travis and Jackie?"

"Maybe Jackie, but Travis don't do that type of work anymore."

"I thought robbing banks was how Travis made his money," Nick said.

"It is; but he said that he will never walk in a place and try to take it at gunpoint. To him, it is much easier to hack into their computer system."

"Who did you have in mind?"

"You two, naturally; and I was thinking about reaching out to the X Man."

"You tell the Colonel that you were gonna ask me?"

"He didn't want me to because, and I quote, 'Nick is into this whole gangster thing these days'," Monika laughed.

Once Xavier agreed to join the team, it was set. The team assembled in McAllen, Texas; and after doing some additional recon on the bank, they were ready to go.

"Mission assignments," Monika said. "We maintain radio silence; other than Jackie calling the plays from the command center."

"Understood," Xavier said.

After Monika reviewed mission assignments for the op, Nick had a question. "What about local police involvement?"

"That's where Rain comes in," Monika said and looked in her direction.

"I was just wondering," Rain said, "since you, Nick, and X Man are going in, and you didn't give me an assignment."

"Your job is the most important."

Rain's job was to create a diversion on the other side of town in order to draw the police. Monika spent the next few days giving Rain a crash course in the safe setup and detonation of explosives. Once Monika deemed her ready, they selected a target; the Feed Warehouse in nearby Mission, Texas.

On the day of the operation, Rain set C-4 in the warehouse and then drove an SUV loaded with the explosives into it. That part went off without issue. It was what happened after that that caused the problem.

After detonation, Rain's assignment was to get into the second car that she had waiting and drive to the bank in McAllen on Highway 83 to cover her teams' exit from the bank; but it was pouring, and she lost control of the car on the wet road. Rain went into a spin, skidded backwards into a curb, and blew out her two back tires.

"Shit!" Rain shouted when she got out and looked at the tires. Rain tried not to panic and figure out how she was going to achieve her objective. She started running and hoped for the best. It wasn't long before she saw a limousine-styled taxi. Rain readied her weapon and ran toward it. She got in the car and shoved her gun in the driver's face. "Take me to South 10th Street in McAllen or die." But now she was stuck in small-town Texas traffic.

Once again, Rain looked at her watch. "Shit!" Rain shouted. "How far away are we?"

"About two miles."

Rain dug in her pocket, pulled out some money, and tossed it at the driver. Then she got out of the car and started running again.

Meanwhile, outside the bank and unaware of the problems Rain was having, the rest of the team prepared to take the bank. Once Nick, Monika, and Xavier entered the bank, each had a primary responsibility. Once all of the bank's employees were cleared from behind the counter and out of the offices, Nick was to go for the money, Monika was to get the manager and get the information that they wanted from the safe deposit box, while Xavier covered the room. What the team's intelligence and reconnaissance didn't tell them, was that four of the men that were in those offices were armed men that worked for the cartel to prevent this type of thing from happening.

"It's time," Monika said and grabbed her weapon. "Remember; maintain radio silence."

"Understood," Jackie said. Nick and Xavier followed suit and the team exited the van and entered the bank.

"Everybody down on the floor!" Nick yelled as he and Monika moved to clear the offices. The operation went south from there. When Monika tried to clear the cartel's men out of their office, they opened fire on her right away.

The first shot hit her in the leg, and Monika returned fire as she limped out of the line of fire. Hearing the shots and seeing Monika go down, Nick and Xavier opened fire on the cartel's men.

While Xavier fired away, Nick made his way to Monika and pulled her to deeper cover. "You all right?" Nick asked.

"My leg," Monika replied.

Nick quickly checked her leg. "Only a flesh wound."

As the cartel's men moved out of the office and continued firing. Nick ripped the sleeve off his shirt and wrapped it around Monika's leg. Xavier kept shooting until he made his way to Nick and Monika. "Where did these fuckers come from?" Xavier asked.

"I don't know. None of the intel I got said anything about this," Monika said as she reloaded her weapon.

"We gotta get outta here!" Xavier shouted.

"No!" Monika shouted back. "We gotta complete the mission."

"Fuck the mission. We have got to get outta here," Nick repeated.

"Nick is right, Monika," Xavier said. "We are outmanned and seriously outgunned."

"The Colonel is counting on us," Monika said.

"The Colonel will benefit from the accurate intel we're gonna give him when we get outta here," Xavier said.

While the debate raged inside the bank, Rain made it to the van. She was tired and out of breath. "What's wrong with you?" Jackie asked. "You're supposed to be outside covering their exit from the bank."

"I know, but I got a flat and had to run here," Rained managed to say.

"Okay ... go ahead and catch your breath, and then get out there. They've been in there too long, Rain. I think something went wrong."

Rain took a deep breath, and then she left the van and headed to her cover position outside the bank. As she got closer, Rain could hear the shooting inside. Rain made it to the door and looked inside. She could see the people lying on the floor with their heads down as the firefight took place all around them.

Rain took out her second gun and entered the bank blasting. She looked around for her team; they had taken up position behind the counter and were taking heavy fire from the cartel's men. "Shit!" Rain yelled and opened fire on the cartel's men. Noticing that Rain had come in and joined the firefight, Nick and Xavier resumed firing.

As the shooting continued, Rain began to make her way toward Nick. "You two all right?" she asked.

"We're fine, but Monika's been shot," Nick said.

"Where is she?" Rain asked.

Nick and Xavier looked around and then looked at one another. "I know where she is," Nick said.

"So do I." Xavier said. "She's gone to the vault to hit that safe deposit box so she can complete her mission."

"I got her," Nick said.

"No!" Rain shouted. "You two keep them busy. I'll get Monika," she said and moved out. With that, Nick and Xavier opened fire to give her cover.

While Nick continued shooting, Xavier reloaded. "You know what this reminds me of?"

"Istanbul," Nick replied and stopped shooting. Xavier nodded his head. "So what are you saying?"

"That you and I need to man up and complete our part of this mission."

"The money."

"If for no other reason, so we have something to show for our troubles today," Xavier said with a sneaky smile on his face.

By that time, Rain had made it to the vault. As expected, Monika was in there. She had identified the box and set the explosive to open it; but she was a little weak from the blood she had lost. When Rain got there, Monika was sitting on the floor with the detonator in her hand.

As quickly as she could, Rain pulled Monika out of the vault and took the detonator from her. But before she pressed the button, Rain broke radio silence and called Jackie.

"Omega. We're in trouble. I need you to drive the van through the front door."

"Repeat your traffic, Delta."

"Drive the fuckin' van through the fuckin' door now, Jackie!" Rain said as she pressed the detonator.

Hearing the radio traffic from Rain, Nick, and Xavier hurried to complete their task and get to a safe position.

Once the box was open, Rain removed the contents. Now that she had gotten what they came for, Rain turned to Monika. "Can you walk?"

"Yeah," Monika said, and Rain helped her get to her feet as Jackie drove through the front door of the bank.

While Jackie covered them with an AK47, Nick and Xavier got in the van with the money. Rain and Monika kept shooting as they made their way to the van. While Nick went to help Rain with Monika, Jackie got back in the van and prepared to leave. Xavier covered for them as Nick and Rain got Monika in the van.

"Get us out of here, Jackie," Xavier said as he got in. Jackie dropped the van in reverse, backed into the street and drove them out of there.

Chapter Two

For Mike Black it was the best of times and yet at the same time, it was the worst of times. His beloved Cassandra was found alive on an island in the Caribbean by Monika and Travis. On a mission that was totally unrelated, Monika discovered a laptop, which confirmed for her beyond a shadow of a doubt that it was not Shy that Black had found beaten and bloody.

The day before the DEA agent was killed at Black's Paradise in Freeport, one of DEA agent Pete Vinnelli's operatives accidentally left the papers detailing his drug operation and the congressional officials involved. After they left Shy picked them up and was looking at them when they came back to get them. She didn't know what it was about, and she hadn't read enough to put it together. The operative told Sally Fitz, and he told Vinnelli before Black killed him. But by that time Diego Estabon, who had kidnapped Shy, had released her; so Vinnelli planned to kidnap her again. However, before Vinnelli could put his plan into action Diego was killed and DeFrancisco was arrested.

Vinnelli and his associates still needed to know what Shy knew and if she had told Black anything, but DeFrancisco insisted that he kill Shy. That's when Vinnelli planned to replace her, frame Black for her murder, and find out what she knew.

Now that she was back, Shy was jealous of Black's relationship with CeeCee, her relationship with Michelle, and the fact that they have a son. Now that she was free to actually see that he had moved on with his life, that he had basically replaced her with CeeCee, she decided to take Michelle and move to Baltimore with her mother.

As for CeeCee, she had always been very insecure about Shy. Now she was heavier than she'd ever been in her life because of her rough pregnancy and as hard as she tried, she couldn't seem to drop that weight. It had already put a strain on her relationship with Black. That and the fact that she'd lost interest in sex during pregnancy and it hadn't returned.

Now Shy was back and CeeCee was devastated. She was sure Black was going to leave her and go back to Shy. So she had isolated herself from him and hadn't actually talked face-to-face with him since the night he told her that Shy was alive and had taken Michelle from her. When CeeCee learned that her mother was sick, she took Mike Jr. and went to New York City, leaving Black alone on the island with Jada West.

Jada's attitude throughout has been; "Your family situation does not and should not have any bearing whatsoever on our business and personal relationship."

So as both Shy and CeeCee played their games of attempted manipulation, Jada was the same uncomplicated businesswoman she'd always been. They were business partners with benefits. But if she chose to be honest with herself, Jada would have to admit that she had fallen very deeply in love with Black. A fact that she never admitted to him or anybody else, and that included herself.

As for Black, he was still desperately in love with Shy. He didn't want to hurt CeeCee; and the way Jada was playing it, she was not going to be a problem. All he wanted was Cassandra back.

So it's the same thing every day. Each morning he would call CeeCee and speak with her mother. "Good morning, Mrs. Collins."

"Hello, Michael."

"How are you this morning?"

13

"Not bad for an old gal."

"How's my boy?"

"He's a good boy. Doesn't cry much. Just sits there looking at me with that smile."

"That's my boy," the proud father said. "And that's why I call him Easy."

"You're right about that. This boy is easy like Sunday morning." Mrs. Collins paused before moving on. "Can I ask you something, Michael?"

"You can ask me anything you like."

"I notice when you call that you don't ask about Cameisha anymore."

"To be honest with you, Mrs. Collins, I know she doesn't want anything to do with me, much less hold a conversation with me. You know that I tried for weeks to talk to her. She would be there and just wouldn't come to the phone. I don't know what else to do. I can't change the way things are. I know it hasn't been an easy thing for her to deal with, but I was hoping that we would be able to work our way through it, but that was wishful thinking on my part."

"I understand, Michael. I really do. But I wish that you could do something."

"What's wrong?"

"I think ... let me stop ... I know that girl is on the wrong path and getting in with all the wrong people again. And she's head strong; won't listen to a word I say."

"When you say, 'wrong people', you mean people like me?"

"No. You're a good man, Michael."

"I understand." Black laughed. "I would be more than happy to talk to Cee if she'll talk to me."

"Thank you, Michael. I know that I can count on you to do what's right."

"There is something that you can do for me," Black added.

"What's that?"

"Would you talk to your daughter and see if she'll let me have my son for a week?"

"When you coming to get him?"

"Whenever she says it's cool."

"Michael, you are this boy's father. As far as I'm concerned, you can come get him any time you want."

"What about Cee?"

"What about her? She ain't got time for this boy. Too busy running the streets. I think the only reason she took him when she came back to the city was because she knew you wanted him, not her." Mrs. Collins laughed a bit. "That and to keep him away from your wife."

"No kidding."

"Don't tell her I said that." She paused. "That is if she ever speaks to you again."

Black laughed. "Your secret is safe with me."

"I take care of this boy every day, so if I say you can come get him, you can come get him and you leave Cameisha's silly behind to me."

"Thank you, Mrs. Collins. I'll be up there to get Easy Mike the day after tomorrow."

"I'll have him ready."

After ending the call with Mrs. Collins, Black called Cassandra at her mother's house. "Good morning, Mrs. Sims."

"Good morning, Michael. And how many times do I have to tell you to call me Joanne?"

"Sorry, Joanne, I promise to do better."

"That's alright. It just shows that Emily raised you to have respect for your elders."

"She did."

Joanne laughed.

"So, how are my girls today?"

"Michelle is outside playing, and her mama is still in the bed as usual."

"Well, put Cassandra on the phone."

After a while, a still half-sleep Shy said, "Hello."

"Hello, sleepyhead," Black said.

Shy sat straight up in the bed. "Morning, baby ... I mean, Michael." The sound of his voice was always enough to bring her out of a sound sleep.

"So I ain't your baby anymore?"

"No, Michael, my baby is outside playing. You and I are good friends who just happen to have a daughter."

"That is where you are wrong. You are my wife."

"So Wanda told me last week. She said that even though I was declared legally dead, since neither of us filed for divorce, we are still legally married," Shy mused.

She was still very much in love with Black and wanted him back in her world, but she wanted to be swept-off-her-feet again; and Shy wanted to make it clear to CeeCee that Mike Black *is* her man and she *was* just a placeholder.

As they did every day when he called, they talked for hours. The difference in this conversation was that this time Black had a plan working, and had questions for Shy to make sure his plan worked.

Two days later when Black arrived in New York to pick up Easy Mike, CeeCee was purposely not there, so Black had a long talk with CeeCee's mother before leaving with Easy. After that, he went straight to Baltimore to Joanne's house. He got there late in the afternoon, so not only was Shy awake, but she answered the door to see Black with Easy in his arms.

"Oh," Shy said and took Easy from his arms. "He is so precious."

"Say hello to your other mother, Easy."

"You mean the woman who should be your mother," Shy said and kissed Easy several times. "Does your woman know you got her son down here with me?"

"I told you, Cassandra, Cee hasn't spoken a word to me since I told her you were alive."

"So how did you get Easy?"

"I have a good relationship with her mother."

"Yeah, right. You probably got her wrapped around your little finger like you got my mother," Shy said. "So, Michael, tell me, what are you doing here?"

"I was hoping to—"

Just then, Michelle came in the room. "Daddy!" she screamed and came running toward him. She jumped in his lap and covered his face with kisses. "I miss you, Daddy."

"I miss you, too, Michelle." Black turned to Shy. "At least somebody here is glad to see me," he said, and Shy rolled her eyes. "You gonna say hello to your brother?"

Michelle jumped down from Black's lap and went over to Shy and Easy. She kissed her brother on the cheek. "Hi, Easy," she said and quickly returned to her father's lap. "Are you here to take us home, Daddy?"

"I would love to, Michelle, but that's up to mommy."

"Mommy, are we going home with Daddy?"

"No, Michelle, we can't. At least not yet."

Michelle buried her face in her father's chest. "That's a very big step for Mommy, Michelle, so I need you to be Daddy's big girl and give Mommy time."

He glanced over at Shy and she mouthed the words thank you. Since she had taken Michelle and come to Baltimore, Michelle had been very vocal about the fact that she was not happy there because she missed her daddy.

"I do have something I want to ask mommy, but I'm afraid that she'll say no."

"Please," Shy said. "The Mike Black I knew isn't afraid of anything. So what do you want to ask me?"

"I was hoping that the four of us could spend the week together at the beach in Ocean City."

"Can we, Mommy? *Can we*, Mommy? Pleeeeeeeeease, Mommy, can we go to the beach with Daddy?"

Shy looked at Michelle and then to Black. There was nothing in the world she wanted more, but she still insisted on playing hard to get.

"I don't know, Michelle," she said, and Michelle started to cry.

"Pleeeease, Mommy. I'll be a good girl, I promise."

"And I promise to be a good boy," Black said.

Shy smiled and looked at Easy Mike. "What about you? You gonna be good, too?"

Easy Mike touched her face and then he kissed her. "Well, if you all promise to be good, how can I say no."

So the Black family spent the week at Ocean City, Maryland and by the end of the week, Black was sure that Shy was ready to come back to him. But Shy hadn't moved in her position. "I'm just not ready yet, Michael."

With that, he took Easy home to CeeCee and returned to Nassau, and into the waiting arms of Jada West.

Chapter Three

Shy was bored. She was a hustler, always had been. It was in her blood. So sitting around her mother's house playing with Michelle and hanging out with her mother's friends playing bridge was getting old quick.

One afternoon she received a letter from Jack. He was the only surviving member of her old crew. Jack got caught in the shootout with E's fake cops and was arrested when the real cops showed up. He'd heard that she was alive. In his letter, he told Shy that he had done his time and was set to get out, and asked if she would be there to meet him when he did. Shy agreed to pick him up.

The only problem was explaining to her mother and Michelle. "Baby, mommy needs to go to New York for a few days to see an old friend," she began as her mother looked on.

"Is my daddy gonna be there?"

"No, Michelle, Daddy is not going to be there. And mommy needs to go alone," she said, and Michelle ran off. "She is so spoiled when it comes to her daddy." Shy shook her head. "My Daddy, my Daddy; she begins every sentence with my Daddy," she said mocking Michelle.

"I don't understand," Joanne said. "If you're just going to see an old friend, then why can't you take her?"

Shy gave her mother a look.

"See, that's what I'm talking about. You don't need to see any of those old friends of yours. Does Michael know what you're doing?"

"No, Mommy, Michael doesn't know, and I would appreciate it if you didn't tell him. I just need you to keep Michelle for a couple of days."

"I will watch Michelle for you, but I got a bad feeling about this, Sandy. You don't need to be getting involved with these people again."

"I am just going to meet an old friend who's getting out of jail, Mommy. No big deal. I mean it's not like I'm going up there to get a package and get back to work," she said and thought about what it would take to actually make that happen, and then quickly pushed those thoughts out of her mind.

A week later, Shy found herself in Rome, New York, sitting in the car she'd rented outside of the Mohawk Correctional Facility waiting for Jack to be released.

When Jack woke up that morning, it was way too early. The sun wasn't even up yet, and try as he did, Jack could not go back to sleep. So he simply laid on his bed and waited for the officers to come get him.

When the time came and his name was called, Jack wanted to run up outta there, but he had spent the last five years building his rep and there really wasn't any point in crashing the work he had put in now. He was getting out and when you get right down to it, that really was all that mattered.

Once he was outside the facility, Jack looked around for Shy. He saw a woman get out of a Ford Focus and started waving at him. He figured that must be her and started walking toward her. As he walked, Jack couldn't help but think back to the last time he saw Shy; the night they found out that not only had E betrayed them, but that he was responsible for all of their problems. For weeks, they had been getting robbed of most of the product and all the money.

Even though she had been waving to him, Shy wasn't sure that the man walking toward her was Jack. If it was, he had lost a lot of weight. Jack was always a big guy. He stood six feet five inches tall, and the last time she was with him he weighed over three hundred pounds. Shy smile when she thought how despite his size, Jack was always well dressed and had a way with the ladies.

"Hey, Jack," Shy said and gave her old friend a hug.

"What's up, Shy?

Shy stepped back. "Look at you, all slim and fine looking."

"I know you don't think I look good in prison issue?" Jack laughed.

"I'm talking about how much weight you lost."

"Seventy pounds."

"Seventy pounds?"

"Nothing to do there but lift weights and read," Jack said as they got in the rental.

"I heard you could have been out three years ago," Shy said as she drove back to the airport in Syracuse.

"I could have. But I thought about having a PO to report to; him trying to violate me at every turn." Jack shook his head. "I didn't want no parts of that. Better for me to give the state what I owe and walk away from them a free man and not owing them shit."

"I know what you mean."

"I guess you do. I mean it wasn't like you was in jail, but you were a prisoner just the same."

"Worse. At least you weren't alone and cutoff from the world."

"I can't even begin to understand what that must have been like for you."

"And you don't want to."

"Well, we are both free now," Jack said and touched Shy's hand. "It's good to see you."

"It's good to see you too." Shy squeezed his hand. "So what do you want to do first?" Shy looked at Jack and thought about what she'd said. "We can see what kind of clothing stores they have at the airport when we get there. That should hold you until we get back to the city."

"Thank you."

"At least you'll look good enough to travel with." Shy laughed.

"Don't want to be seen with me in prison issue?"

"It does kind of scream, look at me, I just got out of jail."

Upon arrival in the city, Shy was as good as her word. She took Jack shopping and bought him a new wardrobe. "Where you get all this money? You ain't got back in the game, have you?" he asked and hoped she'd say yes, she had just been waiting for him to get out to step things up.

"No," Shy said quickly. "Michael puts money in an account for me, so money is never an issue for me." Sure, she had it to spend, but Shy felt like there was nothing like making her own money and controlling her own destiny.

"Sorry that ain't going the way you want it to," Jack said as they walked back to the car.

"Yeah, but it's going the way it needs to for right now," Shy said and thought about their week at the beach. *It was a wonderful week*, she thought, and her mind drifted off.

Shy couldn't have asked for a better time together. For the first time since she'd been back, Shy felt like they were a family again. *Michael was so sweet and attentive to me*, she thought, and a smile washed across her face. Michelle had her daddy and she was surprised at how quickly Easy took to her. He followed her around everywhere she went. If they walked anywhere, Easy insisted that Shy hold his hand, and her lap had become his favorite spot. At first, it made her a little uncomfortable; she wanted him to be her son and not

CeeCee's. But by the end of the week she felt like he was her son.

At the end of their wonderful week together, she told Black that she just wasn't ready to jump back into their relationship like nothing had happened even though that was exactly what she wanted to do. She wanted to be swept off her feet again by the man she loved, and here he was, sweeping her off her feet again. So what was the problem?

"Can't be going all that bad, the way you're smiling," Jack said to end the trance Shy was in.

"Maybe," Shy said and quickly changed the subject. "So what you want to do now? Eat or get laid? Or do you have that handled?"

"No, unfortunately I don't."

"You ain't flipped on me, have you?"

"Oh, hell no! I just ain't got it like that out here," Jack said.

"Tell you what, let's get something to eat and then I'll take you someplace where you can handle your business."

"Sounds good."

After dining on a 20 ounce, dry aged T-bone at Prime & Beyond on East 10th Street, Shy took Jack to Doc's and saw to it that he was well taken care of. When he was done taking care of his business, Jack came and sat next to Shy.

"Thank you," he said.

"So, what do you plan to do now that you're out?"

"Honestly, I only know how to do one thing."

Shy understood because that was her situation too. The only thing she knew how to do was sell drugs. When Jack asked her if she still had any connections, Shy could only think of one person.

Chapter Four

The following day, Shy made a few calls before she went to pick up Jack. "Where we going?"

"To see an old associate," Shy said and started the car.

An hour later, they were in Yonkers and parked in front of the private club where Angelo Collette did business. Like Jack, Angelo had just gotten out of jail after being found not guilty of conspiracy to commit murder.

"You ready for this?" Shy asked. She had never taken anybody with her when she went to see Angelo back in the day when she used to buy product from him.

"Just surprised to be here, that's all."

"Don't be. This is meant to be an introduction. That wouldn't be necessary if I were planning on getting back in, and planned on maintaining control of the contacts."

"That was the way it used to be."

"True. But I'm not getting back in, so there is no need for me to maintain the contacts," Shy said and got out of the car. After receiving the customary reception, Jack was relieved of his gun and they were escorted inside.

"Shy!" Angelo shouted with outstretched arms. "I don't know about you mooks, but she looks pretty good for a dead woman," he said, and hugged and kissed Shy on the cheek.

"How have you been doing, Angelo?"

"Doing good."

"Angelo, this is the man I was telling you about." Shy looked at Jack. "Jack, this is Angelo Collette."

"It's an honor to finally meet you, Mr. Collette," Jack said and shook Angelo's hand.

"I hear good things about you, Jack. Always have. And it's Angelo." He turned back to Shy. "Let's talk in my office."

"I heard that you had some legal issues of your own," Shy said as they walked.

"Yeah, but fortunately there ain't a jury in Westchester County that will ever find me guilty of anything."

"That's good to hear," Shy said and sat down when they reached his office.

"Damn, it's good to see you again, Shy. When Mikey told me that you were alive, I thought that he was just yanking my chain, but here you are in the flesh."

"I couldn't think of anybody else to come to with an issue like this," Shy said.

"Yeah, well, are you sure you want to do this?"

"Like I told you when we talked; I'm just doing a favor for an old friend," she said and looked at Jack.

Angelo too was looking at Jack. "Jack, would you excuse us for a minute? I need to talk to Shy alone."

"Go ahead, Jack. I'll be fine," Shy said, and Jack reluctantly left the office.

"I'm gonna ask you again, Shy, are you sure you want to do this?"

"And I'll tell you again, I'm only here to make an introduction."

"I have heard that shit from so many people, right before they got back in. I know how this thing goes, Shy; it's in your blood."

"That may be true for some people, but I can tell you honestly, I am not getting back in the game."

"Does Mikey know what you're doing?"

"No, Angelo. Michael does not know what I'm doing, and I would prefer that you didn't mention it to him."

"I tell you what, Shy; if Mikey asks me a question I'm gonna answer him honestly. And when he asks me why didn't I tell him, I'm gonna say that you asked me not to. I won't lie to him, but I won't call him as soon as you leave."

"That's fair enough."

Angelo shook his head and wrote down a number. He handed it to Shy. "Have Jack give this guy a call when he's ready."

Shy looked at the paper. "Nicolò De Luca."

Chapter Five

Meanwhile, CeeCee had joined a gym, got herself a personal trainer, and was starting to look and feel like her old self. She looked in the mirror and thought that all she really had to do was to stop eating everything that Bernadette put in front of her.

"But it was so damn good."

But she still wasn't ready to see or speak with Black. Each time he called, she told her mother to tell him she wasn't home; and she was never there when he came to pick up their son.

As she applied her makeup, CeeCee glanced over her shoulder and noticed that her mother was standing there shaking her head. "What?" CeeCee asked.

"Nothing. Just wondering where you were going?"

"I'm going out to have a drink with my girls."

"Really? Well, if you're going out, who is going to take care of this baby while you're gone?"

CeeCee took a deep-exasperated breath. Her mother could be so difficult sometimes. "Could you please watch the baby while I'm gone, Mommy?"

"I don't mind keeping Easy," she said, and CeeCee cringed. She hated the nickname that Black had given their son. "That's what I'm here for; to help you in any way that I can. And he is such a good boy; it's no problem to watch him. I just think that out of common courtesy that you could ask me and not just assume that I'll do it."

"Yes, Mother," CeeCee said and rolled her eyes.

"I mean, you spend all day at the boutique and then you stay out all night with God only knows who. You never have time for this boy."

"I do have time for him," CeeCee insisted. "I do spend time with him. Maybe not as much time as you think I should ... but I do."

"If you say so. But from where I'm sitting, it's me that has time for this boy and who spends time with him."

"If you say so, Mother."

"And what about his father?"

Once again, CeeCee rolled her eyes. "What about him?"

"That man has been calling here every day trying to talk to you, but you won't even come to the phone."

"Me and him have nothing to talk about."

"You know, sometimes I wonder how I raised such a stupid child. Of course, you two have something to talk about. You need to talk about this baby. He is a good man and he is trying to do right by you and this baby. The least you could do is talk to him."

"When did you become a fan of his? I remember when you thought that I was crazy to even be talking to him, much less have his baby."

"That was before I got to know what a good man he is."

"That man doesn't care anything about me. All he cares about are his children and his wife. There isn't any part in there for me to play," CeeCee said and grabbed her purse.

That was a conversation that they had many times before, and she didn't feel like having again. "I will see you in the morning," she said and headed quickly for the door.

As she sat waiting for her girls to come get her, CeeCee began to come to grips with the fact that her entire relationship with Mike Black was a fluke. They were never meant to be; he never loved her. Sure, he needed her to accomplish certain things that he wanted. First, to get his wife's killers, and then to help raise Michelle. But it was never about her.

29

With that realization, CeeCee now understood that, though she was there when he bought it, he really didn't buy that house for her. It was only by chance that she was with him when he got shot. Had she not been there, she would have never been in a position to get close to Michelle. CeeCee knew that Mike Black was never her man; she never was Mrs. Cameisha Black, as she had begun calling herself. All she had was a baby she never really wanted, for a man who never really wanted her. As her girls pulled up in the car, CeeCee understood that she was just a placeholder, holding down the spot until the real Mrs. Black returned to claim what was rightfully hers.

Mrs. Collins stood in the window and watched as her daughter got in the car and pulled off. It wasn't a minute later before a taxicab stopped in front of the building and Mike Black stepped out.

"*Now* he gets here," she said and went to let Black in.

She had arranged for him to pick up Easy that night and had hoped that CeeCee would be home for a change, so they could talk.

She opened the door before he rang the bell. "Evening, Mrs. Collins," Black said with a hug and a kiss on the cheek.

"How you doing?" she asked and went to get Easy ready to go with his father.

Once again, Black headed straight to Baltimore to be with Shy and was surprised that she was not there. Joanne was very vague about her whereabouts. When he left, he took both of his children with him back to Nassau, which was what he had planned all along; but he'd planned on Shy coming with him.

Chapter Six

CeeCee was enjoying herself out drinking with her friends, but in the back of her mind, she kept hearing her mother's words.

You know, sometimes I wonder how I raised such a stupid child. Of course, you two have something to talk about.

CeeCee took another swallow of her drink and hoped that the alcohol would force those thoughts from her mind. It didn't work. No matter what, she could not escape it.

"Hey, CeeCee. Ain't that BB over there at the bar?" one of her girlfriends said and pointed.

"Where?"

"Dah, at the bar."

"That looks like him."

"Thought he was dead like the rest of them."

"I guess not."

Billy Banner a.k.a. BB was the only surviving member of The Commission that was once headed by Bruce Stark. After K Murder and Cash Money, who used to be CeeCee's man, were murdered by Mylo's hit team, BB took off with as much money and product as he could. Now he was back in the city and looking to get back in the game. When BB saw CeeCee he immediately rushed over to her table.

"I thought that was you," he said.

"Hey, BB," CeeCee said.

Since nobody invited him to join them, he pulled up a chair and sat down anyway. "I thought you were dead?" one of CeeCee's girlfriends asked.

"What made you think that, cutie?"

"My name is Jamila."

"Okay, Jamila, my bad."

31

"Anyway, I thought you were dead since the rest of your crew is dead, and ain't nobody seen you in years."

"That's how you stay alive in my line of work."

Jamila rolled her eyes. "What line of work is that?"

BB turned away from Jamila and looked at CeeCee. "How you been, CeeCee?"

"Doing great."

"Heard you was Mike Black's baby mama now."

"You heard correct."

BB stood up. "Let me holla at you for a few ticks."

CeeCee got up and followed BB away from the table. "What's up?" she asked.

"I was wondering if your man was still thinking about killing me?"

"He was never interested in killing any of you. He was never y'all's enemy."

"He wasn't? Then why did he kill Cash and K?"

"He didn't. Your boy Mylo had them killed."

"What about Stark and Moon?"

"I don't know who killed them, but it wasn't Black and them," CeeCee told him, because as far as she knew, they didn't. But the truth was that Bobby Ray and Nick Simmons had killed them when they found out that it was Stark who was supplying Rain in her drug operation.

"That's good to know."

"So what happened to you?"

"After Cash and K got popped, I thought the best thing for me to do was to get out of the city and lay low for a while."

"So what you doing back?" CeeCee asked. She wanted to ask him if he had finally grown some balls, but thought better of it.

"Since Leon killed Rico the area is wide open."

"So I heard."

"See Leon, being more businessman than gangster, is satisfied with the money he's making and doesn't want to draw the attention of law enforcement."

CeeCee seemed bored by this entire conversation. "Smart man."

"But that left the streets wide open and everybody and his pops is trying to get a piece."

"Good luck with that."

"Thanks. So if you're looking to make some money, you might be interested in backing me."

Her first reaction was to scream, *Oh, hell, no!* But the more CeeCee thought about it, the more the idea intrigued her.

Her logic: *If Mike Black is so in love with that drug-dealing bitch he calls a wife, I'll become one. Maybe then he'll love me.*

"Let me get back to you about that," CeeCee said, and then she saw somebody else standing by the bar that she hadn't seen in years.

His name was Byron Winter, but everybody called him Blunt. He and CeeCee used to date years ago before he went to jail. Him, she wanted to talk to.

"Let me get back to you about that," she said again. "But I think we might be able to do something. But right now, if you'll excuse me, I see somebody that I need to holla at," CeeCee said and got up.

"How can I get in touch with you?"

"I'll find you." CeeCee walked away from BB and headed straight for the bar. She stood directly in front of Blunt; he had to do a double-take when he saw her standing there.

"Cami?" he said, calling her by the pet name he had given her when they used to date. He thought about hugging her, but thought better of it. He had heard that she was now Mike Black's woman and had no desire to incur the raft of Black like so many before him.

"Wow, nobody has called me that in years."

"Damn, you looking good, Cami."

"Thank you. You looking pretty good yourself. How long you been out?"

"Two years now."

"That long, huh? I didn't know that."

"Yeah, Cami, it's been that long. I heard you had a baby. Congratulations."

"Thank you."

"Are there wedding bells in your future?"

"No, me and the father are not together anymore."

"I'm sorry to hear that." Blunt laughed. "Shit, let me stop lying. I'm actually glad you ain't with that nigga no more."

"Why is that?"

Blunt leaned closer. "Because as soon as I saw you, I began thinking about us getting back together."

"Really?"

"Really. Mike Black's loss ... and it is definitely his loss fine as your ass still is ... will be my gain."

"So you know who he is, and you're not scared of him?"

"I wouldn't use the word scared 'cause I ain't scared of shit."

"Of course not. What word would you use?"

"Cautious. I know fuckin' with Mike Black is bad for a nigga's health. But I gotta say; you are worth the risk."

"You think so?"

"Oh, no doubt."

"About which one; me being worth the risk or that he is bad for your health?"

"Both."

CeeCee laughed for what seemed like the first time in months and it felt good. "I know fine as I am that I'm worth the risk. But what makes you say that messing with him would be bad for your health?"

"Are you kidding me?"

"No. I'd really like to know."

"Okay. Let me tell you about your man."

"Ex," CeeCee said quickly. "Ex-man."

"Cami; that is music to my ears. But let me tell you about your ex-man."

"The floor is yours."

"You know that he used to work for André Harmon, right?"

"Back in the day."

"Who you think killed André?"

CeeCee rolled her eyes. "Go on."

"After that Chilly ... you remember him don't you? ... took over, and he and Black formed what everybody called the 'dead zone,' because Black wouldn't let anybody do business there. Him and Chilly co-existed for years because he respected the dead zone, until Black had him killed."

"Hold up. If he respected the dead zone, then what makes you think that he had Chilly killed?"

"I don't know why; but I know that his boy Nick and that one-eyed assassin he rolls with killed Chilly."

"My question is why?"

"I told you I don't know; but trust me, Cami, he ordered that hit."

"Okay," CeeCee said skeptically. "Who else?"

"You remember D-Train?"

"Yeah, I remember that bastard. But didn't his girl, Melinda, kill him?" CeeCee asked.

"First of all, she used to be Black's woman, and second of all, do you really believe that she killed him? And if she actually did, it was on Black's direct order."

As CeeCee looked on in disbelief, Blunt told her that Black either committed or was responsible for the deaths of Birdie and his partner, Albert Webb. "And then he wiped out The Commission and half the niggas that was involved with them when he thought they were involved in his wife's murder."

"The bitch ain't dead."

"What?"

"Nothing."

"Then he executed some of Cash's boys."

"They tried to kill him," CeeCee said quickly. She knew that for a fact because she was the one Black turned to, to set them up.

"Now how you know that, Cami?"

"I just know. Just like you know, I know too. And how you know all this anyway? Wasn't your ass in jail?"

"I know because it's common knowledge and word gets around, especially in jail."

Just then, the DJ announced last call for alcohol.

"So what's up, Cami; you gonna let me take you out?"

"Sure, we can go out some time."

"When?"

"You can start by taking me to breakfast."

"Great."

"Let me tell my girls that I'm riding with you," CeeCee said, and walked away thinking that this was who she really was. CeeCee had always been a baller's woman, and Mike Black was too big a step up for her.

ROY GLENN

Chapter Seven

It was getting late when Black got to his house in Nassau with his children. As soon as the car came to a stop, the front door swung open and his mother, Emily, came rushing out. She missed her grandchildren and wished that things would return to some semblance of normal, so she could be with them every day. But she didn't have much hope of that happening.

Both Shy and CeeCee seemed to be pretty intractable in their positions, which she completely understood.

"Cassandra comes home after the ordeal she went through and finds her husband and daughter with another woman, who just had a baby," Emily said to Black one night. "And poor CeeCee. Just had a baby and your wife comes back from the dead."

"Whatever," Black said. "They didn't have to take my children. We could have worked something out."

Emily started laughing. "Work something out? Like what, son? What did you have in mind?"

Unfortunately, Black still didn't have a solution and that bothered him. He considered himself to be a solution-oriented type of guy.

Here's the situation ... boom, boom, boom ... all right, here's what we're gonna do.

But not this time.

"Why don't you just shoot them both and take your kids?" was the question Bobby had asked him, and Black gave him the finger. "Ain't that how we solve the majority of our problems?"

"Did you shoot Pam?"

"I damn sure thought about it," Bobby said.

Knowing that it wasn't that simple, Black contented himself to make the best of the bad situation. For the time, he was enjoying having both of his children together.

For the next week, Black would spend the day with them, and once they were asleep, he would go to work. His first spot was The Grill. He would stay there for a few hours, and then he would head for Paraíso for a couple of hours before heading home, so he could get some sleep, because Michelle always woke up early.

Black had just arrived at Paraíso and had sat down in the spot that he and Jada usually sat like king and queen, proudly surveying their empire, when he saw Jada.

At first, she smiled that beautiful smile like she was glad to see him, and then her eyes narrowed, and her fists hit her hips. Then she started walking toward him with fire in her eyes. Black stood up to greet her.

"Good evening, Ms. West. You look beautiful this evening."

"Whatever, Mr. Black. I know that your children are here, and I understand and respect that, but I am feeling just a bit neglected and I don't like it, not one bit."

Black laughed a little. "You want to go upstairs and take care of that right now?"

Jada closed her eyes, took a deep breath, and visions of Black ripping that six thousand dollar Emilio Pucci printed gown from her body and ravishing her appeared.

"Yes," she said, and then she opened her eyes and exhaled. "But we are not going to start that."

"Just trying to help, Ms. West."

"And believe me, I appreciate and want your help with this matter. But I am still convinced that conducting those activities here at our place of business, sets a bad precedent."

Black laughed. "We run a ho house. Everybody in here is fuckin' but us," he said, and Jada looked horrified.

"This is not a ho house, because my ladies are not ho's," Jada said and took a playful swing at Black. "Just call me at Sandy Port in the morning."

"I can do that."

"Now I think you should leave before I change my mind, and drag you upstairs and ride your face like a cowgirl in heat," Jada said and walked away quickly.

Black laughed. "Whatever you say, Ms. West."

It was after four in the morning when Jada finally left Paraíso and headed home to her condo at Sandy Port. So when the phone began ringing just after nine, it was way too early. Jada started to ignore it, but she remembered telling Black to call her in the morning. She smiled thinking; *He must want to be inside of me as badly as I want to feel him inside of me.*

"Good morning, Mr. Black."

"Can I speak to Jada West, please?" a female voice requested. Since it was early and she didn't recognize the voice, and it wasn't Black on the other end, Jada had a bit of an attitude.

"Two questions. Who is this? And how did you get this number?"

The female started laughing. "Girl, you still a fool," she said and laughed again. "Girl, this Love."

"Love?"

"Yes, Jada, it's Love. We went to high school together. When you was dirt-broke and fucked up, you used to sleep on my floor."

"Oh my God. Love, is that really you?"

"Yeah, bitch, it is really me. And believe me, it wasn't easy tracking you down since you all big-time now and shit; getting this number wasn't easy, either."

"I know it couldn't have been. How are you, girl?" Jada asked, and a flood of memories, both good and bad, crowded her mind.

"Girl, I been doing good."

"Are you still working at the tattoo parlor?"

"Jada, let me tell you; I still work there, but I am part owner now."

"That is great," Jada said. And for the next hour and a half, she and Love talked about old times. Even though she was happy to hear from an old friend, Jada still wondered how Love got her number. "So how did you get this number anyway, Love?"

"I was doing a tat for an old friend of yours and she gave me the number."

Now Jada was beyond curious, wondering what old friend had her number in Nassau. "Who?"

"You remember a woman named Chante?"

"Yes," Jada said, and then it made sense. Chante was actually a cop named Rachael Dawkins. And even though Jada hadn't spoken with Chante in years, it didn't surprise Jada that she knew how to reach her.

"Well, she been getting tats from me for years; so when I told her that I needed to get in touch with you, Chante rattled off your number."

"Oh," Jada said and thought, *She knew the number by heart?* "So why did you need to get in touch with me, Love?"

"Girl, I almost forgot. Your mother is out of jail."

"What did you say?"

"Your mama is out of jail and she been asking about you."

41

After getting some information, Jada rushed Love off the phone, got out of bed, and went to fix herself a drink. She sat out on her deck and thought about her parents, which was something that she didn't allow herself to do. Her mother used to boost from the mall and commit identity theft with checks and credit cards. But if push came to shove, Jada's mom would do whatever it took to make money. "Honey, when you got a man's back, I mean truly got his back, a woman gotta step up. Sometimes a woman gotta use what she got to get what she gotta get to take care of her family."

She remembered that her mom would give it up for money if she felt she needed to, and how it used to piss her father off. There were many times over the years that Jada wondered how those words, *Sometimes a woman gotta use what she got to get what she gotta get*, had influenced her decisions.

Then she thought about her father. When she was seventeen, he had a woman who was giving him money, and he would bring the money home and would give it to her mother. That's just how they did it. But one night the woman followed him to their apartment, and she waited for him to come out. Jada was watching from her bedroom window and saw the woman walk up, put a gun to his head, and kill him.

After that, her mother had to go for herself. She went out and got herself a job and worked it for two weeks, before she accidentally slipped in the ladies room. She sued them and got a little settlement, but her plan was to do what she called "washing the check." That's when they use isopropanol to erase the amount on the check, and then put in a new amount. She got a fake ID and setup an account to run the checks through, and went for it.

42

However, the insurance company knew who they'd sent the check numbers to. So it was easy for them to match her work ID with the bank's surveillance video. With only a court appointed lawyer at her side, the judge gave her ten years.

For the first couple of months after they took her mom away, Jada wrote her once a week. But she never got an answer to any of her letters until one day when she got one from her that simply said that she should stop writing her. Her mother said that reading her letters was too painful for her, and for her not to even think about coming to see her, because she didn't want Jada to see her like that. Now she was out and wanted to see her.

Chapter Eight

Rain sat alone in her office waiting for Nick to return her call. She'd been calling him for an hour and hadn't gotten a call back. While Rain waited, she began watching the movie she had just downloaded, Black Girls Get Nasty Too with Beauty Dior and Ayana Angel that made her think back to how her relationship with Nick began.

Although Rain had heard about him just about all of her life, she had never met Nick until the night that she walked into what used to be her father J.R's, office, and there he was. As soon as Rain saw him, she knew exactly who he was; and knew that she wanted to get with him. If for no other reason, she wanted to hear firsthand about all the things that he and his old partner Freeze had done. Over the years, the pair had become legendary in some circles. And the fact that she thought that he was fine as hell, moved her that night in ways she didn't think were possible. But despite all that, Rain played hard.

Nick and Rain went after the people that had robbed his spot together, and the games began. They went after one of Rain's people, a man named Shake and Rain killed him. She caught him with one to the gut and one to the head. Rain was hyped as they drove away from there.

Since that night, Rain did everything she could to make her presence known to Wanda. And eventually, she found out and confronted Nick, and they broke up. Rain had Nick all to herself then, or at least that's what she thought. But Wanda had a way of keeping her hand in and that annoyed Rain to no end.

On that particular night, Rain was upset that Nick had become more attentive of Wanda, since the attempt on her life. Tired of waiting, Rain started to leave the club, and as she was passing the bar, she ran into an old boyfriend named Ronnie King, the son of Robert King. After Black killed André Hammond and Jamaica killed Cazzie Riley, Jimmy Knowles, and Charlie Rock, Vincent Martin attempted to kill Black. That started a war between Black, and what remained of André and Cazzie Riley's organizations. Once Black was successful in eliminating his enemies, Chilly took over what was left of André's drug operation, and Robert King took over Cazzie Riley's drug operation. In those days, Robert was good friends with Rain's father; JR. Rain had known Ronnie as long as she could remember. They even dated for a while before he went to jail for an assault charge.

"What's up, Rain?" Ronnie asked.

"What you doing here?" Rain asked.

"Is that anyway to speak to the nigga you used to say you loved so much?"

"Two things." Rain signaled for the bartender. "One, I was a young, stupid bitch in love those days." The bartender placed a drink in front of her. "Two, I got over that shit quick. Something about them other stupid bitches you were fuckin', and then your ho-ass went to jail."

"But I'm out now."

"So."

"I told you the last time I saw you that I wanted you. So when can we get together?"

Rain laughed. "I told you I got a man, and that we run this place."

"So you got a man. What that mean to me?"

"I'm not having this conversation with you again," Rain said.

"So where is this man of yours?" Ronnie asked.

"He's ...," Rain began; and that's when she was reminded that she had no idea where her man was. She was sure that Nick's disappearance had something to do with Wanda.

"See," Ronnie said and laughed. "You don't know where that nigga is, do you?"

"You know what, Ronnie ... fuck you," Rain said and started to walk away.

Ronnie grabbed her by the arm and Rain started to reach for her gun. "Hold up."

"What?"

"Where you going?"

"Away from you."

"Don't be like that, Lorraine."

"Don't call me that," Rain said and took a swing at Ronnie.

"Why, that's your name?"

"'Cause I don't like it," Rain said quickly.

"Okay, okay. Look, let me make it up to you. Come ride with me and I'll buy you a drink."

Rain looked at Ronnie like he was stupid, and then looked around. "We at a bar. A fuckin' bar I own. I can get all the drinks I want. What I need to go with you for?"

"'Cause you don't know where your man is; and coming with me can be your way of getting even. Even if he don't know about it."

Rain shook her head and walked away. "You coming?"

Ronnie smiled and walked to her. "Anything you wanna do, other than get a drink?"

"Let's see how the drinks go first."

They left J.R's and Ronnie walked Rain to his car. He let her in, and then walked around and got in.

"Where we going to get this drink?" Rain asked. Ronnie reached in the backseat and grabbed a bottle. "Patrón?"

"For sure. You think you know me."

46

"I used to Rain. I used to love you."

"Yeah, and when you was twelve, you had big zits on your face, but you got over those too." Rain laughed.

"I did look bad, didn't I?" Ronnie laughed along with her.

As Rain sipped Patrón and laughed with her old boyfriend, her mood began to change, and she began to relax. That was until Ronnie drove through an area that Rain was familiar with.

"Turn right here, Ronnie."

Ronnie smiled and made the right turn as Rain requested. As they drove down the street, Rain saw what she was looking for, but hoped she wouldn't see; Nick's car parked down the street from Wanda's house. When they passed by the house and she saw there were no lights on, Rain felt her blood boiling.

"Take me back to my spot," she demanded.

Ronnie looked over at Rain and smiled. "What's wrong?"

"Nothing. I just remembered some shit I gotta take care of."

Chapter Nine

After returning Rain to her spot as she requested, Ronnie returned to his father's office. He went in the office and knew that his little move was a success. "You all are still talking?"

"No," Robert said and stood up. "I think we are just about done here."

Bobby glanced over at Nick and Wanda and then stood up. "I think so, too," he said to Robert and reached across the table to shake his hand.

Nick and Wanda stood up.

"I hope this old man didn't waste a lot of time, but I felt like with all that was going on that we needed to talk."

"It was time well spent, Robert."

"I just needed some assurances, that's all," Robert said and walked Bobby to the door.

"Not a problem. I assure you that we have no interest in reentering that market," Bobby said.

"That is good to hear, Bobby. You tell Black that I said congratulations on the boy."

"I will," Wanda said. And after handshakes and another round of assurances, Bobby, Nick and Wanda left the office.

"Biggest waste of an hour I ever spent," Nick said as they all got in Wanda's car.

"Home," Wanda told her driver before turning her attention to Nick. "I was starting to feel like I was going to be sick if we had to cover the same points again."

"You two need to learn some patience," Bobby said.

Nick and Wanda both laughed. "Okay, Mr. Patience," Wanda said and laughed some more. "I wanted to slap you when you said it was time well spent."

"It was. And what's blowing me is that you two gangsters don't see it," Bobby said and looked at Nick. He started to say, *That's why Mike took the reins of power from you,* but thought better of it.

Nick stopped laughing. "What you mean, Bobby?"

"It was time well spent because now we know that the Kings got something going, and it doesn't involve us. And he wants to keep it that way."

"Now that I'm thinking about it, he was trying to feel us out. See what our plans are."

"Is that why you played stupid every time he asked what we were doing, or what Mike has going in Nassau?" Wanda asked.

"I knew you two would catch on. Y'all a little slow sometimes; but with a little guidance you get it," Bobby said.

"I'll make some discreet inquiries," Nick said. "See what I can find out."

"Good," Bobby said and thought about the situation.

Robert King had gone through Wanda to arrange a meeting with Bobby. He wanted to meet with Black. Wanda put him on hold and called Black in Nassau.

"What I want to or need to meet with that guy for?" Black never did have much respect for Robert. "No. Talk to Bobby and see if he'll meet with that nigga," Black told her. Since he wasn't interested in talking to Robert, Wanda told him that Black was out of the country.

She setup the meeting for her and Bobby to attend. That night, unknown to Wanda, Bobby told Nick to meet him at Wanda's house. When Wanda opened the door, Bobby informed them both that they were going to the meeting with him.

Neither objected.

At the meeting, Robert, in more detail than was necessary, pointed out that Black's organization had backed Leon in his move against Rico. Bobby quickly pointed out that Rico's men made an unsuccessful attempt to kill him and Black, and that the threat was dealt with.

"That may have given you, and possibly others, the impression that we were backing Leon, but nothing could be further from the truth," Bobby assured.

After that, Robert insisted that he get assurances that Black's organization had no intention of moving into the void that was left by Rico's death. Bobby assured him several times that was not their intention.

Ronnie was at the meeting when it started, and then Rain began blowing up Nick's phone. "Who is that?" Bobby asked.

Nick looked at Wanda. "Rain."

"What you looking at me for?" Wanda whispered and smiled. "I never blew up your phone like that."

"Maybe you wasn't putting it on Wanda the way you putting it on Rain," Bobby said softly.

Nick laughed.

"Fuck you, Bobby!" Wanda said.

"I've heard that before."

Overhearing that conversation, Ronnie excused himself from the meeting and went straight to J.R's to get with Rain.

Ronnie stood in the window and watched them drive away. His father came and stood next to him.

"I hope wherever you went and whatever it was that you rushed out of here for was productive, son."

"From a point of view it was, or will be productive," Ronnie said and hoped that it would. Either Rain would be his or she'd become his source of information on what Black's people were doing.

"Good. I know what a ho you are, so I was hoped you didn't run off to go pray at the temple of the open thighs."

"No, Pop, nothing like that," Ronnie lied. He was dying to get back in between Rain's thighs. *That pussy is so damn good.* "So, how did the meeting turn out?"

Robert told Ronnie what was said and the outcome of the meeting. "In the end, Bobby assured me that they are not moving to get back in the game."

"You believe him?"

"I've known Bobby Ray a long time. If his intention was anything other than to stay out of the market, he would have told me he was getting back in and dared me to do something about it." Robert patted his son on the shoulder. "We have nothing to fear from them," he said and returned to his desk.

"I wasn't scared of them niggas."

"No; just careful, right?"

"Right, Pop."

"I usually am about these things."

"I'm gonna start making moves to consolidate and take over the area."

"No."

"No?" Ronnie questioned. "I thought we talked about this."

"We did; and what I want you to do is bring in some outside muscle to be the face of the takeover. Allow them to be very violent in how they go about it, and when things are where we want them to be, then we step back in."

At first, Ronnie was reluctant to go along. He had been planning this takeover the entire time he was in prison. But Robert convinced him that it is better to control things from the background.

"I made a call to a friend in Cleveland. He promised to send some good people," Robert said.

Chapter Ten

At 7:30 P.M., Delta flight 4166 arrived from Cleveland at
New York's John F. Kennedy International Airport. Once all
the other passengers exited the plane, Monk got up and
made his way down the aisle.

"Have a nice day," one flight attendant said.

"I hope you enjoyed your flight," the other attendant
said as Monk passed.

"Best two hours I ever spent," Monk said as he left the
aircraft. When he got to baggage claim, he stopped and
looked around. It wasn't too long before a man approached
him.

"Mr. Monk?"

"Who's asking?"

"My name is Stanley. Mr. Robert King sent a car for
you."

"Good," Monk said and quickly handed the man the bag
he was carrying and began walking toward the exit.

Stanley took out his communicator. "We're on our way
out."

"Got yah," Duke, the driver, said and started the car.

Once they were outside, Stanley stepped forward. "Right
this way, Mr. Monk," he said, and led Monk to a waiting
limousine. Duke opened the door for Monk.

"Good evening, Mr. Monk. My name is Duke; I'll be
your driver this evening."

"Nice," Monk said and got in the limousine. When
Ronnie spoke to him, he said he would have somebody pick
him up. Monk just wasn't expecting this.

"Duke is one of our best drivers," Stanley stood outside
and said. "He's a professional, discreet driver; and Duke is
ready to attend to any need, Mr. Monk."

"I like that." Stanley stepped away from the door and Duke started to close it. "Where're you going, Stanley?"

"Up front, Mr. Monk."

Monk shook his head. "Sit back here with me."

Stanley and Duke looked at one another. "Yes, sir, Mr. Monk," Stanley said.

Monk slid over and Stanley got in. Duke shut the door and made his way around to the driver's side. "Base, this is Duke. Departing JFK," he said. "Destination; King Family Restaurant."

"Acknowledged. Current drive time from JFK to destination is 45 minutes," the dispatcher advised.

"Acknowledged. Suggested route?" Duke asked because it was required.

"Van Wyck Expressway to 678 North to I-95 North. Take exit 12 on the left to merge onto Baychester Avenue."

"Route accepted."

"Tell Stanley—" she started, and Duke quickly cut her off.

"No can do, base. Stanley is in the back with the client," Duke said slowly for impact.

"Oh."

"At the client's request."

"Oh."

"Acknowledged, base."

Meanwhile, Monk and Stanley rode in complete silence, and Stanley wondered why Monk asked him to sit back there with him. Then about thirty minutes into the trip, Monk broke the ice. "What do you do for Mr. King?"

"I manage his limousine service."

"Manager, huh?" Monk said. "So King owns this?"

"Yes, sir," Stanley said and went into his sales presentation. "We know you book limousine services because you want something special, and we have it just for you. We deliver a quality service in smooth, clean, and luxurious vehicles, coupled with a support system that ensures safe and on-time limousine service. When you book with us, you have access to well-maintained executive sedans, stretch, and limousine buses for corporate travel.

Monk laughed a little. "Is that a fact?"

"We have a large fleet of stretch limos, SUVs, and specialty vehicles. Along with these, efficient limousine service to and from all New York area airports; we provide an enormous variety of specialty limousine services in and around the New York area for proms, formal homecomings, weddings, bachelor and bachelorette parties, concerts, sporting events, and more."

When they arrived at the restaurant, Stanley led Monk to where the Kings were seated. Ronnie stood up when he saw them coming.

"Gentlemen, this is Mr. Monk."

Ronnie shook hands with Monk. "Have a seat," he said, and Monk took a seat at the table.

"How was your flight?" Robert asked.

"Good."

"And the trip from the airport?"

"Good trip."

"Excellent," Robert said. "Now, let's get down to business. As you know, our business is a very competitive one. And from time-to-time there comes a need to eliminate some of that competition."

"That's me; I am a problem eliminator. Just tell me who and where to find them."

Ronnie slid a piece of paper in Monk's direction. "There's a list of names."

Monk picked up the paper and read over the names. "Tree and Ramos Hurley, Antonie Edmonds, B Money, Donald Henderson, Sly Stone."

"Here's some background information," Ronnie said and slid a file across the table.

Monk picked up the file and thumbed through it. He looked up at Robert. "Wanna know anything or you just want it done?"

"Just get it done. In that order, if it's not too much trouble," Robert said.

"I'll take care of it," Monk said and stood up.

Chapter Eleven

When he left the restaurant, Duke took Monk to his hotel. He sat down on the bed and took out the list and the file he had gotten from the Kings. It was pretty detailed; like they hired a private investigator to follow each of the targets. Addresses, known associates, security strength, hangouts, recommendations and tactics for how and where to take them; it was all there. The longer he looked over the information, the more he understood that the Kings had planned to do the work themselves. There was a part of Monk that wanted to know why they'd backed away. At the same time, part of him didn't care. He was getting paid. And getting paid quite well for this work. He went to the mini-bar, got a couple of bottles of scotch, and got to work.

By morning, Monk had gone through all the information. He took a quick shower and headed out to look things over for himself. When he returned to the hotel that evening, Monk had made a determination about where and how he wanted to do it, and which of his men he was going to bring in to do the work.

"Don't need all them niggas," Monk said out loud. He could always call for more if he needed them. He picked up the phone and called back to Cleveland to get the men he needed to New York.

"Barkley's."

"This Monk. Is Bailey there?"

"Hold on."

Ten minutes later, Sonny Bailey came to the phone.

"What's up, Monk? How's it going in the rotten apple?"

"Got some work. You interested?"

"Shit, yeah."

"Get here as soon as you can and bring Dylan and Mobley with you."

"Hardware?"

"Bring the van."

"Take about nine, ten hours to drive there."

"See you then."

Once his men arrived in the city, they wasted no time in getting started with their task. Their first target was Marvin "Tree" Hurley and his brother Ramos. According to the information Monk got from the Kings, they liked to hang out in a bar on Boston Road named X-Pressions.

Monk and his men went to the bar and waited for Tree to arrive. Once he was there, two of Monk's men tricked him into a back room. They threw a rope around his neck and started to choke him.

Bailey tightened the rope around Tree's neck. Tree struggled to get free as Dylan stood in front of him and punched away at his gut. Monk stood back and watched. Then he stepped up. He got in Tree's face.

"Call your brother. Tell him to come up here to meet you."

Tree didn't answer him. Dylan hit him three times in the face. "Answer the man."

"Fuck you!" Tree yelled.

"Call your brother or I'll kill you," Monk said, and Dylan pointed a gun at Tree's head.

Tree understood all too well that he was going to die that night. If he called Ramos, they would both be dead.

"Fuck you," Tree said again and spit in Dylan's face.

"Kill him," Monk said.

Bailey pulled the rope tighter; Tree struggled against it for as long as he could. Slowly his body stopped moving.

The rope was pulled from his neck and Tree fell to the floor. Dylan kicked him. "Fuck you!"

"How we gonna get Ramos here?" Bailey asked.

"Go out there and grab one of them working girls and bring her here," Monk said, and Dylan and Bailey left the back room. When they closed the door, Monk dragged the body behind a desk, just as Dylan and Bailey returned with a woman. Dylan pushed her toward Monk. He slapped her and held a gun to her head.

"I want you to call Ramos. Tell him where you are and that somebody just killed Tree. Got that?"

"Yes," she said through tears.

Monk handed her the phone and she did as she was told.

Ramos Hurley was well-known for his temper and as soon as he got the call, he jumped in his car and drove straight to X-Pressions. When Ramos rushed in the bar; Monk was standing by the door. Ramos was shot, point-blank in the side of the head.

A TALE OF THREE WOMAN

Chapter Twelve

Three days later, Antonie and his crew were at a party for his uncle's sixty-fifth birthday. When the party finally broke up early that morning, Antonie, his partner Dip, and four women went looking for a restaurant that was open. Antonie and two of the women headed to his new Infinite convertible; Dip and the other two women headed to his new Infinite coupe. "Where we going?" Dip asked.

"Just follow me," Antonie said and got in his car. Dip got in and they drove off. Monk and his men followed them in a van and two stolen cars.

They drove around and found place after place closed. The group finally made their way to Pelham Bay Diner on Gun Hill Road.

Antonie, Dip, and the ladies got out of their cars and walked toward the diner. Monk's men pulled up alongside them and started shooting. Dip was hit immediately with several shots to the chest. Antonie hit the ground as the women screamed and ran for cover. Knowing that he was the intended target, Antonie got up and ran for his car, drawing fire away from the innocent women. Monk's killers trained their guns on Antonie and kept shooting. Antonie hoped he could make it to his car and get away. He collapsed and died next to his new Infinite convertible.

Chapter Thirteen

It was 7:30 A.M. when Kirk arrived at the crime scene. His new partner, Marita Bautista, was already there when he got there. They had been working together for a while now, and were just starting to get a feel for how the other liked to operate. Bautista was a little intimidated by Kirk's considerable reputation. As for Kirk, he was intimidated as well. Not by his new partner's wealth of police experience, but by her appearance. Marita Bautista was a beautiful Latina woman with a fiery temper and a strong desire to be considered a good cop by her peers.

She's a good cop, Kirk remembered telling his buddy, Sanchez, one night. *But she is so fuckin' fine that sometimes I can't concentrate from looking at her.*

"Morning, Bautista."

"What's up, Detective? Glad you could join us," Bautista said and laughed a little.

"What do we got for us today?"

"This is Sylvester Jackson aka Sly Stone, and that is Tammy Banks. They were both tied and executed. Neighbor heard the shots and called it in," Bautista told Kirk.

"Any sign of forced entry?"

"Yeah, crime scene boys are working on that and I got uniforms canvassing the building."

"Good work; you've covered all the bases."

"Mind if I ask you a question, Detective?"

"That's what I'm here for."

"This is the third drug dealer of some note that's been murdered in the last couple of days."

"And?"

"I'm wondering if there is some type of pattern developing."

61

"How so?" Kirk asked. He was thinking the same thing; but decided to play devil's advocate with his new and inexperienced partner.

"B Money was just leaving the apartment of one of his mistresses in Crown Heights, Brooklyn," Bautista began, "when a red and yellow van pulled up alongside his parked Cadillac. Gunmen opened fire from inside the van. B Money took five shots to the face and neck at close range. He died at the scene."

"What else you got, Bautista?"

"Bruce Franks aka Bruno was found in his car outside a restaurant. He took a shotgun shell to the back of the head. And when the officers opened the trunk of a car they found the naked body of Donald Henderson aka Big D. He'd been stabbed, strangled, and brutally beaten. Multiple twenty-dollar bills had been stuffed into every orifice of his body."

"That is meant to be a symbolic gesture that it was greed that killed him."

"You see the pattern?"

"Yes. But there have been two others that the captain dropped on me this morning."

"Who you got?"

"Tree and Ramos Hurley. And Antonie Edmonds. Their bodies were found at a bar called X-Pressions on Boston Road. Tree was strangled and his brother, Ramos, was shot point-blank in the side of the head. Three days later, Antonie Edmonds and his partner, Dip, were shot to death outside the Pelham Bay Diner on Gun Hill Road."

"Yeah, I'd say there's a pattern."

"And what does it tell you, Detective?"

"That somebody is eliminating drug dealers."

"The question for us is why, and the why will tell us who," Kirk said. "So who would benefit from this group of slime being out of the way?"

Chapter Fourteen

Shy had just put on the finishing touches to her makeup, when her cell rang. She looked at the display. "Michael," she said aloud. Since she had spoken with him earlier, Shy was pleasantly surprised that he was calling at that time of day.

"Good afternoon, Mr. Black."

"Good afternoon, Mrs. Black. How are you?"

"I'm fine."

"Did I catch you at a bad time?"

"It is never a bad time to talk to you. But I am getting ready to go out soon."

"Where're you going?"

"Me and an old friend I ran into, Jackie, are going shopping; and then we're gonna get something to eat," she lied. Shy didn't like lying to him, nor was she ready to explain why she was waiting for Jack to pick her up, so they could make a drug deal with Angelo's contact, Nicolò De Luca.

"I won't keep you then, Cassandra. Enjoy your afternoon," Black said and started to end the call.

"No," Shy said quickly. "You are never keeping me. Believe that. Whatever else I got going can wait."

"You sure?"

"Yes, Michael. I would much rather talk to you then do most things in this world.

"Most?"

"Yes, most. There are some other things that I enjoy doing."

"Really?"

"Really. But most of those things I'd want to do with you anyway."

Black held the phone. Sometimes he didn't understand her. Here she was talking like being with him, like their time together was important. He started to ask, *If that was the case, why aren't we together?* "Like what?" Black asked instead.

Now it was Shy looking at the phone like the person on the other end was crazy. "I can think of one or two things off the top of my head." Shy closed her eyes and thought about the week they'd spent together at Ocean City and what a great time they had with the children.

"Like what?"

She also remembered how good the sex was between them. "I'll tell you when I see you," Shy said. Just that morning she woke up wanting to feel him inside her. "It's so quiet, Michael. Where are the children?" she asked to change the subject.

"Easy is asleep and Michelle is in her room playing."

Shy's cell began to vibrate. "Hold on, Michael. I got a text message coming through. She glanced at the message: I'M OUTSIDE.

"That's Jackie. She's outside," Shy said grabbing her purse and heading for the door.

"Then I will let you go."

"I won't be gone for long. Can you call me back? I want to talk to Michelle. I miss her."

"She misses you."

"Has she asked about me?"

"Yes," Black lied. "She asks about you all the time."

"That's good to hear. Listen, I'm about to get on the elevator so I will talk to you tonight."

"I love you, Cassandra," he said to dead air. Either she'd lost the signal, or the feeling wasn't mutual. Either way, he was glad to get her off the phone before he had to lie to her again. Truth was, it was CeeCee that Michelle had been asking for; but he recently learned that when it came to women, some things were best left unsaid.

Shy stepped off the elevator and walked outside of the hotel where Jack was waiting. She too, was glad to end the call; because if he'd asked her anymore questions, everything she'd say would probably be a lie.

"What's up, Shy?"

"Hey, Jack," Shy said, still thinking about her family and her desire to be with them. "How's it going building a new team?" she asked, more to take her mind off her family than anything.

"Don't worry, I got that handled. But I wanted to ask you something."

"What's that?"

"Are you sure that you want to get involved in the business again after all you've been through?"

Shy didn't answer right away since she had been asking herself that same question and to that point, didn't have an answer to give.

"I would think that after all you've been through ... kidnapped twice and shit ... that sitting around quietly with your mom and your daughter, would be just what you'd want to do," Jack said. "And what's up with you and Black? I know he still loves you by the way he calls you all the time."

"Honestly, Jack, I would think that too. I sat around with my mom for weeks playing Bid Whist and Bridge with her friends; listening to them tell old stories, talking about men, and asking me when am I getting back with that husband they've heard so much about. Jack, I was about to lose my mind."

"I can only imagine," Jack said as he drove down the FDR.

"While I was alone on that island for all those years, to keep from going crazy, I would ... you know ... role play."

"Role play?"

"Yeah, I would imagine myself in situations and talk and act like I was really there. Sounds silly, but it worked. I think that's what kept me from losing my mind."

"What would you think about?"

"All kinds of shit; but I had two favorites. One was being with my family, not no other bitch and her son. Just me, my husband and my daughter."

"That's what you really want."

"Yeah, but I spent more time imagining that I was with you and Tony, God rest his soul; and we were out doing our thing."

"No shit?"

"No shit."

"So where does Black and Michelle fit in now?"

"I know Michael loves and wants me. Right now, he's in Nassau with the kids; and he tells me what a great time they're having and how happy they all are together. And then he tells me how he wishes I was there to share this wonderful moment with them. A part of me wants to be there, but here I am with you, about to go meet a man about some product."

When they arrived at their destination; Paesano on Mulberry Street, Shy and Jack went inside, but her mind was still on being with her family.

While Jack talked to the maître d, she thought that it wasn't too late to turn back, but at the same time, that it was. Shy was confused. Her adrenaline was pumping just like it used to before she did business. She felt the excitement and the lure of the game. For a minute, she was back on the island role-playing. Only difference was that this time, she was playing for real.

Is this what you really want? She asked herself.

The answer was a resounding no. Shy was just about to tell Jack, "Let's go," when the maître d turned to Jack and said, "Mr. De Luca will see you now." And without a word of protest, Shy followed them to a table in the back of the restaurant.

Nicolò De Luca sat in the back of Paesano where he usually held court, and sometimes did business. One of his families' biggest earners, De Luca, also known as Nico Dees, was described as being very energetic and decisive in his work. Nico was someone who exuded confidence. He always wore a white tie and a white carnation with custom-made suits, which made up his expensive wardrobe. He drove flashy cars and had a passion for Broadway showgirls. Nico had an arrest record that included homicide, assault, and felonious assault, but he was never convicted on any of the charges. In his early years, he was into extortion, union racketeering, and illegal gambling operations that included betting on horses and running numbers, until the lure and money from the drug game turned him.

When Nicolò's men saw them coming, they stood up. "Here we go," Shy said as one approached.

He held up his hand. "Mr. De Luca will only talk to her."

Jack started to protest, but Shy stopped him. "It's okay, Jack," she said and followed him to the table.

"Mrs. Black?" Nico asked as Shy got to the table.

"Mr. De Luca."

"Please, call me Nico," he said and extended his hand. "Have a seat."

"Thank you," Shy said and sat down.

"I hope you don't mind me saying so, Mrs. Black, but Angelo said that you were one of the most beautiful women on the planet."

Shy smiled like she had never heard that line before. "I am going to have to thank Angelo for the compliment. And you too, of course."

"Definitely the prettiest woman to grace this place," Nico said, and Shy tried to act like she was flattered by it. She was there to do business and nothing more.

If I needed to hear how pretty I am, I will call Michael.

There was a time when Shy would have taken the time and had fun flirting, but now the idea seemed foreign to her. She was a married woman now, and the game of cat and mouse no longer held any interest to her.

"Well, thank you again. Shall we get down to business?"

"Not much to talk about. Angelo already told me what you want. It's just a matter of working out the details."

"And if it is all the same to you, Mr. De Luca—" Shy began.

"Nico, please, call me Nico."

"Nico," a now frustrated Shy said. "If it is all the same to you for reasons that I'm sure you understand, I will leave my associate to work out the details."

Nico looked disappointed. "I completely understand." He leaned closer. "I usually don't either, but I was willing to make an exception in this case."

With that, Shy stood up and signaled for Jack. "It was a pleasure meeting you. I'm looking forward to a very lucrative relationship between us."

A TALE OF THREE WOMAN

Chapter Fifteen

CeeCee locked the door to her boutique early and brought down the gate. After she put the lock on, she called BB and asked him to meet her at her mom's house. Since she'd been back in the city, she'd been spending less time with her son and more time at the store. Without her knowledge or approval for that matter, her mother had allowed Black to take Mike Jr. back to Nassau with him. He told her it was just going to be for a week. She was surprisingly cool with that. The boy looked just like his father, and each time she looked at him, it was a nagging reminder of Black, and the fact that he didn't want her. So she spent her time at the boutique.

CeeCee opened her boutique with the money she'd gotten the night Cash Money was murdered by Mylo's hit team. When she found the drugs and the money, she quickly packed it up and gave it to a friend in the building before the police got there.

That wouldn't be her only windfall. She also picked up a large sum of money when Black came to her with a plan to avenge his wife's murder. Due to her current situation, she thought about that night many times. At first, CeeCee thought that it was a godsend.

Mike Black came to my apartment and I'm ecstatic. I was really starting to think he wasn't feeling me the way I was feeling him; that he only saw me as a soldier, a pawn on his chessboard, somebody else to use to get things done for him. But there he was, outside my door. I wasn't expecting anybody, and I had just gotten out of the shower and had a big towel wrapped around me, when I heard this loud knock at the door.

"Who is it?"

I peeked out and he leaned in front of the peephole. "Mike Black."

"Don't go nowhere. I gotta put something on."

"Don't go to any trouble," I heard him say, and I stopped to think about it. I peeked again and saw Kevon, so I knew that wasn't happening. I practically ran to my room, thinking what to put on. I knew how much he likes the color black, so I grabbed a black dress and slipped into it. All the while, I'm thinking that all the flirting and hints I'd been dropping had finally paid off. Mike Black was here to see me. I do something quick with my hair, put on just a little bit of makeup because I knew he didn't care for women that wore too much, put on some four-inch stilettos, and I'm back at the door in five minutes.

"I didn't catch you at a bad time, did I?"

"Not at all. I was just sitting around watching TV. Please, come in," I extended my hand gracefully. He walked in and I looked at Kevon. "He's not coming in?"

"He'll be right there if I need him."

"I understand." I smiled and shut the door.

He never goes anywhere that Kevon isn't with him. I'm thinking that since Kevon is staying in the hall, that this visit is personal. I mean, if it was business Kevon could come in, right? Boy was I wrong. "I need you to do something very important for me," Black said to me that night.

"You know I'll do anything for you. Just tell me what you need?"

"I arranged for you to meet with a reporter from the Post."

I frowned. "For what?"

"I want you to give him a story."

I looked at him for a second or two and then I sat back. "This is about your wife, ain't it?"

"Yes."

"I thought so."

"What you know about my wife?"

"I know that she was murdered, and that they accused you of her murder. I know that finding her killers is the only thing that's important to you."

And that's when I should have told him to get out my apartment and come back when he wants me. But I didn't. I went along with it because I'm thinking, she's dead, right? Once he gets whatever this is out of the way, that I would be one-step closer to getting him.

Now, in retrospect, I wished I hadn't lifted a finger to do anything that involved that bitch, because all I have to show for it is my son and that boutique. The problem was that he never knew me ... the real me. When we started out, his first impression of me couldn't have been good. That night I met him, Cash hadn't been dead long, and Angelo Collette was in my face.

And I want you to know me. I want you to know that I'm more than just some gold digging baller's girlfriend.

Now CeeCee felt like she had never gotten past that point with Black. And why should he? That's what she was; what she had always been ... a baller's girlfriend ... and Mike Black was too big a step-up for her.

CeeCee was devastated the night that Black came home and told her that the bitch was alive. There were times when she thought, and friends have told her, that she handled it all wrong. Instead of running and crying when she heard the news, she should have made a stand for her man. That was exactly what she did that night. She locked herself in their bedroom while Black took Michelle to see her mother. *Her mother*, CeeCee thought. "I was her mother!" CeeCee yelled as she drove.

That night, she should have stood up and said, "I'll get the children ready." And when it was time for them to leave, she should have gone right along with him. She should have gone and established that Mike Black was her man now, and told her she should cancel any plans she had of getting anywhere near her man. But she didn't. CeeCee locked herself in their room, and hadn't seen or spoken to him since.

She told herself many times that it wouldn't have done any good. She had always known that Black loved, and was still desperately in love with Shy, when they were together. At first, it didn't matter, but the closer she got to him, it became painfully obvious that he would never feel for her the way he did for Shy. Now she realized just how wrong she was. Mike Black was never her man. She was just holding the spot until Shy came back. CeeCee turned up the music and tried to block all of those thoughts.

When she got to her mother's house, BB was there waiting for her. CeeCee had thought long and hard about what she was about to do. She knew that what she was about to do was only to spite Black. She thought about her son and thought that he deserved better. She didn't understand why ... *Maybe it's that postpartum depression nonsense his mother was trying to run on me* ... but CeeCee still had not bonded with him. CeeCee didn't feel close to him, and for that, she felt bad.

She'd hoped once they got back to New York and away from Black, that she would feel differently and finally bond with her son. But to this point, that hadn't happened, and she couldn't say for sure that it ever would.

"CeeCee!" BB yelled as soon as she got out the car.

"What's up, BB?" CeeCee said, and sat down on the stoop next to him.

74

"Ain't nothing."

"You been waiting long?"

"Just got here."

CeeCee thought about inviting him in, but thought better of it. She didn't want to hear her mother's mouth over bringing "the wrong people" in her house, and she definitely didn't want her mother to overhear any part of the conversation that she was about to have.

She took a deep breath before she began. "I decided to take you up on your offer and go into business with you."

BB began to laugh.

"What's so funny?"

"Nothing. How much you thinking about investing?"

"How much you need?"

"I need fifty grand to make things happen."

"I was thinking about a hundred," CeeCee said, and BB looked shocked.

"Grand?"

Chapter Sixteen

It was another beautiful Caribbean afternoon in Nassau, and as they often did, Black and Jada had lunch together, and then retreated to the room they kept at the Hilton.

They were so good together.

But this time, instead of bolting from the bed and heading for the bathroom, the way Jada usually did after their sex, she simply laid there next to him. Black glanced over at her and started to ask her what was up with that, but instead, he settled into his pillow. He was about to put his arm around her, when Jada sat up in bed and said, "I'm going to New York."

"Business or pleasure?"

"Mostly pleasure, but you know me; I will find a way to mix some business in with it."

"Jada West on a pleasure trip? Say it ain't so," Black said and noticed the thoughtful look that now covered Jada's face.

Jada looked into Black's eyes. "I never told you about my mother, have I?" Jada began.

"No. You haven't. But you haven't really told me a lot about you, Ms. West. As much time as you and I spend together and how much I enjoy that time, at times, you are a closed book," Black told her.

Jada thought about apologizing and promising to be more open, but she knew better. Each time she saw him; each time they were together, the closer Jada felt to Black. And as good as they were together, no matter how good their sex was, Jada knew that in his current situation, it would be best for all parties concerned if she continued to keep the book called *Jada*, closed to him.

Jada took a deep breath. "My mother just recently got out of jail and she's been asking to see me."

"What was she in jail for?"

"She did ten years for washing checks."

"What about your father?"

"My father's dead. Murdered by some woman that he was dealing with. She followed him home to our apartment. And then she waited until he came out, she shot him while I watched."

"I'm sorry. I know that couldn't have been easy for you."

"It wasn't. It felt like all the life had been drained from my body. He and I were so close. And I loved my daddy so much that I couldn't believe what I was seeing. It felt like part of me was dying."

"What was his name?"

"Lucas West."

"I've heard that name before."

"I'm not surprised. Back in his day, my daddy could shoot pool with the best of them. They used to call him sweet stick Luke."

"I knew your father. Not well. Seen him shoot a few times. He was good."

"He was one of the best," Jada said, remembering the days when she was younger and used to go to the pool hall with her dad; and how much pride she felt because her daddy was the best there was with a stick in his hand.

"So you're going to New York to see mom, huh?"

"Yes, Mr. Black."

"When was the last time you saw her?"

"Ten years ago on the day they sentenced her. And before you ask, she didn't want to see me."

"Why?"

77

"For the first couple of months after they took moms away, I wrote to her once a week to keep her up on what was going on with me. I never got an answer to any of my letters, until one day I got a letter from her that simply said that I should stop writing her. She said that reading my letters was too painful for her."

"How did your mother not wanting to see or hear from you, make you feel?"

"I was devastated."

"How old were you then?"

"I had just celebrated my eighteenth birthday when they took her away."

"How did that make you feel?"

"I felt like I was truly alone."

"How long are you gonna be up there?"

"I may be up there for three days, four at most," Jada said. "What about you? How much longer are you going to have your children?"

"Another week, maybe two."

"Perhaps you'll make some time for me if they're still here when I get back."

Black smiled at Jada. "Is anybody meeting you at the airport?"

"I haven't made arrangements yet."

"If you like, I could arrange a limo for you."

"That would be excellent."

Black reached over and got his cell out of his pocket. He dialed a number. "Robert King, please," Black said when the phone was answered.

"Who's calling?"

"Please tell him that Mike Black is calling."

It didn't take Robert King long to come to the phone. "Black, what's up?"

"Robert, how are you?"

"Just fine for an old man."

"That's not what the ladies say, at least that's what I hear."

Robert laughed. "Not me. I left all the ho-hopping to men like you and my son."

"How is Ronald?"

"Ronald is good. If he would listen long enough, he'd actually learn something about this game."

"He'll be learning the game from one of the best," Black said graciously.

"Thank you, Black," Robert said. "Now, I know a man like you didn't just call to blow sunshine up my ass. So, tell me what I can do for you?"

"Two things. First, I wanted to say that I meant no disrespect to you by not excepting your invitation to come and talk. I have a million things going on down here and that was just not a good time."

"Not a problem. As I'm sure you know I met with Bobby; he was able to address all of my concerns."

"That is good to hear."

"What's the second?"

"A very dear friend of mine will be in town tomorrow; she'll be there for three or four days. She'll need transportation and I would consider it a personal favor if you would put somebody good with her."

"Not a problem, Black," Robert said and paused for a second or two. "I thought you had a limo company of your own?"

"I did, but Wanda sold it."

"She should have called me. I would have given you a good price for it."

"I still got a few cars, but that's for the funeral business."

"I see. But like I said, not a problem, Black; you know that. Just get me the details."

"Her name is Jada West. When she has flight information I will have her call you."

"Sounds good."

"I owe you one, Robert."

"No problem, Black. Next time you're in the city, you can buy an old man a drink."

"Deal," Black said and ended the call. He turned to Jada. "You now have a limo and driver at your disposal."

"Thank you, Mr. Black. I love a man who can get things done for me," Jada said and got out of bed and headed for the shower.

The following afternoon at 7:15 P.M., American Airlines flight 2110 arrived at New York's John F. Kennedy Airport. Jada West exited the plane and made her way to baggage claim. When she got there, Jada saw a limo driver holding up a sign that read WEST.

"I believe that it's me you're looking for, sir," Jada said.

"Good evening, Ms. West. My name is Duke; I'll be at your disposal while you're in the city."

"Splendid."

"Do you have any luggage?"

"Yes," Jada said and handed Duke her ticket so he could claim her bags.

"Why don't I escort you to the vehicle, and then I'll come back and pick up your luggage.

Once Duke had collected all of Jada's luggage, he took her to the Peninsula Hotel on Fifth Avenue at 55th Street. She had used that hotel for business for years when she lived in New York and would meet and entertain potential clients at their rooftop bar, Salon De Ning. After Jada checked in, she informed Duke that she wouldn't need him anymore that evening.

"However, tomorrow I am going to want to go uptown to the Bronx."

Duke handed Jada a business card. "Just call that number and I will be waiting when you come down."

"Tomorrow morning, say 10ish?"

"Just give me a call," Duke said, and left Jada for the evening.

Although there was an excellent spa in the hotel that she frequented any time she was in the city, when she got in the car, Jada told Duke to take her uptown. She had made appointments to get some maintenance done. Jada called her old hairstylist, Rewa, to see if she could work her in that day, which wasn't a problem. Once that was done, Duke took her to get a manicure and a pedicure. Now that her maintenance was out of the way, Jada had Duke take her shopping. When Duke saw her coming, he got out of the car, opened the door, and took her packages from her.

"Where to now, Ms. West?" Duke asked expecting to do more shopping.

"Co-op City. Section 3, please."

"Yes, ma'am."

A little more than an hour later, Duke pulled the limo up in front of the building, let Jada out, and then he insisted that he escort her to her destination.

"Well, thank you, Duke. Somebody must have mentioned to you that I am an excellent tipper."

"No, ma'am, nobody mentioned that; but it is good to know."

Duke escorted Jada to the door and knocked.

"Jada?" Love said when she opened the door.

"Hello, Love. It is so good to see you again," Jada said and hugged her old friend. Then she turned to Duke.

"Will there be anything else, Ms. West?"

"No, Duke, nothing else. I will call you when I'm ready to leave," Jada said, and Duke gently closed the door behind him.

"Jada?" Love asked again.

"Yes, girl, it's me."

"Who was that?"

"That's Duke. He's my chauffeur while I'm in town," Jada said. "No big deal."

"It is to those of us who don't have one and can't afford to rent one. Yeah, it's a big deal. But Jada, look at you. Looking like new money," Love said.

Jada was wearing an Armani Collezioni stripe shawl collar jacket; a chic, striped-style suit that featured a unique overlapping shawl and notched lapels; stretch silk satin blouse and Duchess satin pencil skirt, with Jimmy Choo crushed metallic leather sandals.

"All Armani and silk." Love leaned close to Jada. "If you don't mind me asking, how much an outfit like that cost you?"

"Love?" Jada said and looked shocked that she would ask. "Yes, I do mind." Then Jada leaned closer to Love. "About three thousand."

"Dollars?"

Jada giggled. "Just a little something."

"You paid three grand for that outfit?"

"You think I paid too much?" Jada mused.

"For everything you got on," Love said, and Jada stopped her.

"No, Love, that's just for the outfit. It doesn't include the shoes or the accessories. The shoes were a thousand, and I couldn't begin to tell you what all this jewelry costs."

"Stop it, Jada," Love said and hugged her old friend again. "But seriously, girl, just what do you do that you got it all like that?"

Jada smiled. "I am an entrepreneur and my business is recruitment and training," she said. Jada didn't think that Love needed any other answer.

"Whatever it is you doing, please, Jada, you need to hook me up," Love said, not really knowing what she was asking for.

Being the entrepreneur that she was, Jada sized her up. *She still has some shape, but all those tattoos will never do.* "Trust, you don't want any part of this business."

"I don't know; what kind of business is it?"

"Love, I tell you what, I am so glad to be away from it for a couple of days, I can't find the words. But I am going to be here for a few days, so we have plenty of time to talk about that later. I want to talk about you. What about you? You still working at the same tattoo parlor?"

"Yeah, but like I told you, now I am part owner," Love said with a big smile.

"That is great, Love." Jada hugged her again.

"Who would have thought it? Huh, Jada? You and me both successful entrepreneurs."

"I know, right? If the old gang could see us now," Jada said.

"I know. When I tell people that I own the parlor, they can't believe it. Honestly, girl, sometimes I don't believe it myself."

"Speaking of the old gang, you ever see any of them?" Jada asked; and the next hour was spent by the two old friends talking and catching up. And in those two hours, Jada kicked off her heels, took off the jacket, and found out something important about herself. The Jada West that she portrayed to the world was somebody that she and Sasha created. She looked at Love. This was who she really was. Just a girl from around-the-way.

This is why Mr. Black thinks you're a closed book.

But she was sure that she didn't want to do anything to change his perception. *Mr. Black is very much a married man, who is trying to get his family back together.* Jada wondered how much longer would there be a place for her. Sooner or later that woman will come to her senses and go back to her husband.

Jada didn't want to think about that, so she pushed thoughts of Mike Black away. She decided to ask the question that she wanted to ask the moment she walked through the door. "So where is my mother?"

"I haven't seen her since the night before I called you," Love said. "Hopefully, she'll get back in touch with me."

"Do you know where she's staying?"

"No, sorry; I didn't ask her, and she didn't tell me." There was a knock at the door.

Jada looked disappointed. "I guess I'll just have to wait until she gets in touch with you again," she said as Love got up to answer the door.

When the door was opened, Love led her new visitor into the living room.

"Hey, Love. You heard anything from that gal of mine?"

Love extended her hand toward Jada.

"Jada?"

"Hello, Mommy."

Jada bounced up, rushed to her mother and gave her a big hug.

A TALE OF THREE WOMAN

Chapter Seventeen

It was just after 10 o'clock the following morning when detectives Kirk and Bautista arrived at the midtown law offices of Wanda Moore. "Who's office is this?" Bautista asked.

"This is Wanda Moore's office. She's—"

"I know who she is. Wanda Moore is Mike Black's lawyer."

Before becoming his partner, Detective Bautista had heard a lot about Kirk. He was practically a legend. Since her time at the academy, Bautista had heard stories about Kirk and his quest to imprison Mike Black. When she found out that she was going to be his partner, Bautista was excited to have the opportunity to work with him.

"You've done your homework."

"You think Mike Black is behind these killings?"

"Not really."

"Then what are we doing here," Bautista asked.

"I just wanna ask some questions."

Prior to it burning to the ground, anytime Kirk needed to talk to Black he would simply stop by Cuisine; a supper club once owned by Black. If Black wasn't there, there would usually be somebody who could address his concerns and answer his questions. Since the fire, Cuisine has been closed, and to this point, Black hadn't shown any interest in rebuilding or opening another.

"Good morning," Kirk said as he approached the receptionist.

"Good morning, sir. How can I help you?"

Kirk took out his badge and showed it to the receptionist. Bautista did the same. "Detectives Kirkland and Bautista to see Wanda Moore."

"Can you tell me what it's in reference to, Detective?" she asked as she picked up the phone to dial Wanda's assistant, Keisha Orr.

"I just have some questions for her."

"Wanda Moore's office."

"I have detectives Kirkland and Bautista here to see Wanda."

"Ask them to have a seat and somebody will be with them shortly."

Keisha got up from her desk and knocked on Wanda's door. Then she stuck her head in. "Wanda."

"Yes, Keisha."

"Detectives Kirkland and Bautista to see you."

"Thanks, Keisha. Please go get them and escort them to the conference room. Make sure they are comfortable, and tell them that I will be with them shortly."

"Yes, ma'am," Keisha said, and went off to carryout Wanda's instructions. Wanda picked up the phone and dialed a number.

"Hello," a still sleeping Bobby answered the phone.

"Morning, Bobby. Sorry to bother you, but I got Kirk here."

"Kirk," Bobby said and glanced at the clock.

"Anything I need to know about before I talk to him?"

"Not that I know of. But I'll check with Nick."

"Don't bother. I'll call Nick. You go back to sleep."

"Troublemaker."

"What?" Wanda giggled.

"Whatever, Wanda. Call me back and let me know what Kirk wants."

"Will do," Wanda said and ended the call, and then she called Nick.

When the phone rang, Rain woke up first. "Nick," she said and nudged him.

"Huh?"

"Answer your phone."

Nick reached for the phone and looked at the display, and saw it was Wanda calling from her office. He glanced back at Rain.

"Go ahead and answer it," she said, letting Nick know that she too saw the display.

"Hello."

"I know you're laying up with your two-bit ho, so I won't keep you. I got Kirk down here and I wanted to be sure that there is nothing I need to know about before I talk to him. You know how I hate to be blindsided."

"I have no idea why he's there. Have you talked to Bobby?"

"Yes, and he doesn't know, either."

"Let me know if it turns out to be something," Nick said and got ready to hang up.

"Nick!" Wanda yelled.

"Yes."

"You mind asking that lowlife bitch if she has something going that neither you nor Bobby knows about?"

"Hold on," he said and looked at Rain. "Wanda's got Kirk in her office."

"And?"

"She needs to know if you got something going."

"Nope."

Nick nodded his head and turned his attention back to Wanda. "She said no."

"Thanks, Nick," Wanda said and got ready to go to the conference room. She started to call Black and ask him, but she didn't see any point in that. Wanda knew that Black had too much going on with Shy and CeeCee and the children to have anything going. Besides, if he did have something going, he would have told Bobby.

"Good morning, detectives," Wanda said cheerfully when she entered the conference room.

Kirk immediately sprang to his feet. "Good morning, Wanda," he said. "This is my new partner, Marita Bautista."

Bautista stood up and shook Wanda's hand, and then she looked at her usually stoic partner. In Wanda's presence, he was all smiles. *He is practically giddy*, Bautista thought.

"What can I do for you, Kirk?"

"Black in town?"

"He's in Nassau. You want me to get him on the phone for you?"

"What about Nick or Bobby?"

"They are both probably asleep, but I can call them for you too."

"You know it was a lot easier to talk to them when they had businesses open," Kirk said.

"My understanding is that the construction at Impressions is proceeding on schedule and should reopen in the fall." The night after Cuisine was set on fire, somebody set a bomb at Impressions. "Which reminds me, do you have any suspects in either of those incidents?"

Kirk laughed a little. "Now, you know," Kirk began and then he thought about it. "And then again maybe you don't; but the word on the street is that the Villanueva brothers out of Miami were responsible and they have been dealt with."

"Touché." Wanda smiled. "So, Kirk, are you going to tell me what's going on?"

"Last couple of days, five dealers have been murdered."

"And you think that we had something to do with them?"

Kirk stood up. "Just thought I'd ask. You never know."

"You never do," Wanda said and looked at Bautista. She could tell that the whole interaction had the new detective confused. "Do you have a card, Kirk?"

Kirk dug in his pocket and fished out his card. "Here you go."

"I will have both Bobby and Nick get in touch with you."

"Thank you, Wanda. We've taken up enough of your time."

"No problem at all," Wanda said and escorted the detectives to the elevator. "Always a pleasure to see you."

"Really," Kirk said excitedly. "If that's the case, maybe you'll have dinner with me sometime?"

"You have the number," Wanda said as the door closed.

For the entire time that he'd been trying to lock Black up, Kirk had been interested in Wanda. And through all of those years, he never had the nerve to ask her out. For one, he thought she'd say no, and two, he thought that it might compromise his integrity. But he knew that Black had banned Wanda from having anything to do with the illegal side of their business. So now, Wanda was just a lawyer who happened to represent Mike Black.

"Where to now?" Bautista asked once they were in the car.

Kirk looked at his watch. "There is one other person I want to talk to, but it's too early for him too. So, in the meantime, let's go to the Pelham Bay Diner on Gun Hill Road. Antonie and his partner, Dip, were murdered there. Let's check out the crime scene and re-canvass the area, see if we can't pick up any fresh leads."

ROY GLENN

As Kirk drove to Gun Hill Road, Bautista looked at her partner. Since she began riding with Kirk, Bautista had developed what she called "a schoolgirls crush" on Kirk, and now found that she was just a bit jealous.

Chapter Eighteen

Rain could no longer contain herself and decided to confront Nick about the night she thought he'd spent with Wanda.

"Where were you the other night?"

"I told you; I had a meeting."

"Meeting my black ass," Rain screamed. "Try again ... 'cause I know you wasn't at no damn meeting."

Nick's eyes narrowed and he stepped closer to Rain. "What the fuck is your crazy ass talking about now?"

She stepped to his chest. "You know what I'm talking about, mutha fucka."

"No, I don't. And you really need to backup off me and check your tone," Nick said.

Rain could be hard to handle when she got mad like that; but one thing was certain; they always had fantastic sex afterwards. The problem was getting her to calm down and listen to reason.

"Fuck that shit! What you gonna do if I don't? Put two in my head?"

"Keep on and I will," Nick said, looking around for his gun. Not only had her visit caught him by surprise, but her anger as well.

"Looking for your gun? Wanna use mine?" Rain asked. She quickly pulled her gun and handed it to Nick.

Knowing Rain wasn't playing; Nick put one in the chamber. "You wanna tell me what you're so fuckin' mad about?"

"You fucked her; didn't you?"

"Fucked who?"

"I know, you fuckin' so many of these shanks that you don't know who all you fuckin'?"

92

"This is getting us nowhere." Nick gripped the handle of Rain's gun a little tighter. "Just say what's on your mind."

"I know you fucked Wanda that night."

"What night?"

"The night you said you had a meeting with Bobby."

"What about it?"

"You fucked her."

"No, I didn't."

"Yes you fuckin' did, nigga; don't fuckin' lie to me," Rain said and reached for her other gun. Nick put the barrel to her head. "Go ahead and kill me. It don't matter no more. I got nothing left. I know you fucked Wanda more than just that night, and that you fuckin' Mercedes, Danielle and Tasheka."

Since he was actually fuckin' Mercedes, Danielle and Tasheka, Nick didn't deny it. Instead, he told the truth. He had not been fuckin' Wanda, and surely didn't fuck her that night. Even though the subject did come up after the meeting.

After Bobby got in his car, Nick walked Wanda to her door. Nick looked good to her, but in her eyes, he always did.

"I'd invite you in for a nightcap, but that probably wouldn't be a good idea," Wanda said.

"Why wouldn't it be a good idea?" Nick asked.

"I don't think that I have to explain to you what it is that we both know so clearly, Nick. We've known each other too long to play those kinds of games."

Truth was that Wanda was feeling kind of horny; but what she knew better was that she had no intention of simply trading places with Rain. She still wanted Nick; and Wanda could tell by the things he said and the way he still looked at her, that Nick still wanted her.

93

If she allowed him in the house, Wanda knew that they would have sex and she would become the step-off. Wanda had decided long ago that Nick wasn't the right man for her. But the heart wants what the heart wants, and she still wanted Nick.

So Wanda's plan was a simple one; She would do all she could to break Nick and Rain up and expose Rain as the lowlife bitch she was. Wanda hugged Nick, carefully leaving lipstick on his collar, and kissed him on the cheek.

"Goodnight, Nick."

Rain demanded to know where he was the night that she and Ronnie King rolled by Wanda's house. Naturally, she left out the part about Ronnie being with her that night. As far as she was concerned, Ronnie King was old news that no longer interested her. Still, there was no need for her to give up the high ground, especially when there was nothing going on between them. Rain Robinson only had eyes for Nick. The fact that he had fucked Wanda was breaking her heart. She wanted to cry, but that wasn't about to happen.

"Me, Bobby and Wanda went to a meeting that night."

"Try again, nigga! I know that Black banned Wanda from having anything to do with that side of the business."

"True, but Bobby sees that whole situation differently from Black. It was Bobby's idea to bring Wanda along.

"Whatever, mutha fucka. If you was at a meeting, who was y'all meeting with?" Rain yelled more than asked.

Nick was about to tell her, but then he got mad. "Who we were meeting with is of no concern of yours. I did not fuck Wanda that night or any other time. You're just going to have to trust me."

Rain backed off, but still didn't believe him.

Chapter Nineteen

After Rain angrily left J.R's, slamming his office door behind her, Nick decided to call it a night and go home. *Since I'm getting all the grief for it anyway, maybe I should just go fuck Wanda,* Nick thought and laughed as he got in his car and drove to his apartment. When he stepped inside the apartment and turned on the lights, there sat Colonel Mathis.

"Hello, Nick."

Nick had started to reach for his gun, but once he recognized the voice he relaxed. There was a part of him that was surprised to see the Colonel, but Nick knew that he should have been expecting him; had a bottle of Woodford Reserve Kentucky Bourbon and a note telling the Colonel to make himself comfortable.

"Colonel."

"How are you, Nick?"

"You know, deep into this gangster shit, Colonel. What about you?" Nick asked.

"I don't know about you, but I could use a drink."

"Right." Nick gave a half-hearted salute and went to make the two of them a drink. He returned with the drinks and handed one to the Colonel.

"What am I drinking?"

"Kentucky Bourbon."

"If it's Woodford Reserve, you were expecting me."

"No. But it should have been." Nick said and shot his drink. "And since I know you didn't come here to have a drink and talk about old times, what do you want?"

"Same old Nick. No bullshit small talk for you."

"What do you want?"

"Got a job for you, Captain."

"Can I get you another drink? Since my answer is no we can fuck around and have bullshit small talk."

"You haven't heard what the job is, Captain."

"You can tell me about the job if you want to, Colonel, and my answer would still be no. And stop calling me Captain."

"Let me guess; you're about to tell me that you don't do that type of work anymore."

"Not even going to bother since you and I both know that I did that thing with Monika for you."

The Colonel laughed. "So you'll work for Monika, but not me?"

"That's sounds about right."

"What about Travis Burns?"

"What about him?"

"One of your more dependable men, isn't he?"

"What about him?"

"Mr. Burns is a bank robber," the Colonel said and looked to Nick for a reaction.

Tell me something I don't know, Nick thought but remained stone-faced.

"He gains access to his target's network," the Colonel continued. "He studies how to obtain his objective, while attracting as little attention as possible before taking the bank for no more than a million dollars. The FBI is very interested in him. They call him the million-dollar bandit."

"Travis is a big boy, Colonel. I'm sure he knew the consequences of his actions. My answer is still no."

"I hoped it wouldn't come to this."

"Come to what?"

"I was hoping that you would just say, yes sir; what are my orders?"

"That's funny, since I don't take orders from you anymore," Nick said confidently and went to pour another drink.

"That's not entirely true. Captain." The Colonel stood up and took a deep breath. "By order of the National Security Adviser, effective immediately, your commission as captain in the United States Army is hereby reactivated. Your country needs you, Captain."

Nick handed the Colonel his drink. "You can't be serious?" he asked, but the Colonel remained stone-faced. "You *are* serious."

"Relax, Captain." The Colonel took a sip of his drink. "I am not here to return you to active duty; you can still run around here, playing gangster and fuckin' your little gangster girlfriend," The Colonel paused. "If that's what you want. But the world is a dangerous place and it's getting worse every day. Your country invested a lot of money in you; now your country needs those skills."

"Don't have much of a choice, do I?"

"You could shoot me now and go on the run; but short of that, no." The Colonel stood up and started for the door. "Come on."

"Where we going?"

"What?"

Nick stood up and saluted. "Where are we going, sir?"

"What part of *immediately* wasn't I clear about, Captain?"

"None, sir."

"We are going to meet the rest of your team and be briefed."

An hour later, Nick and the colonel were passed through the gates at Fort Hamilton in Brooklyn. The colonel led Nick to a room with two sentries posted outside the door.

"Go on in, Captain, and meet the rest of your team. Briefing will begin at 22:30," The Colonel looked at his watch and walked away.

Nick opened the door and was surprised, but not shocked, to see Monika, Xavier and Travis seated at the table. The one person that he was surprised to see there was Jackie Washington. Xavier and Monika looked up when the door opened, and Nick walked in.

"He got you too, huh?" Monika said.

"The hard way," Nick said.

"What you mean?" Xavier asked.

He sat down. "He reactivated my commission. What about you two?"

Xavier and Monika looked at each other. "He offered me money," Xavier said. "What can I say, Nick? Or should I call you Captain," he said. "I'm a mercenary."

Nick looked at Monika. "I hate to say it, but me too. He told me how much, and I said I'm in. But truth be told, the Colonel ran that same reactivation shit on me over a year ago. That was how he got his hooks back into me." She stood up and saluted. "Lieutenant Monika Wynn awaiting your orders, sir."

Nick looked at Travis and Jackie. "I know how you got here, Travis; but what's up with you Jackie?"

"He said I had certain skills that this team needs. I told him no; and then he told me if I didn't cooperate with him, Travis was going to jail," Jackie said.

Nick looked at his team and slowly began to laugh. "Now it makes sense."

"What makes sense?" Monika asked.

"He didn't need us to hook up to take that bank for him. This is the real objective."

"He wanted the band back together," Xavier said, and everybody laughed.

"So now we know that this job requires a hacker, a getaway driver, a sniper—"

"Munitions and a team leader," Monika added as the door swung open and the colonel walked in.

Clapping. "Very good. Fact of the matter is, there is too much at stake to trust this to anybody else."

"So what's the job?" Xavier asked.

The colonel dimmed the light and an image appeared on screen. "This man is Abd-Al-Qadir, which loosely translated means; servant of the capable and powerful."

"A true believer," Nick said.

"He is believed to be a moneyman for three violent extremist organizations operating on the continent of Africa. Senior American military commanders believe that these groups were trying to forge an alliance to coordinate attacks in the United States and on other Western interests."

"What three groups are we talking about?"

"Shabab in Somalia, Al Qaeda in the Islamic Maghreb across the Sahel region of northern Africa, and Boko Haram in northern Nigeria. To this point, they have not yet shown the capability to mount significant attacks outside their homelands. Each of those three, independently presents a significant threat not only in the nations in which they primarily operate, but regionally. However, recent intelligence has led our analysts to conclude that Abd-Al-Qadir is spearheading an effort to obtain a nuclear device which will present a threat to the United States' interests," Colonel Mathis said. "Usually, reliable sources tell us that they have obtained a sufficient amount of plutonium-238 and a French surface-to-surface, guided missile."

"Milan 2," Xavier said.

ROY GLENN

"Good to know that you haven't forgotten everything," The Colonel said.

Xavier started to give The Colonel the finger, but what he hadn't mentioned to the rest of his team was that three years ago, The Colonel reactivated his commission as lieutenant as well.

"How far away are they from launching?" Nick asked.

"They still need to obtain a targeting system. Once they get that, weeks, if not days." The Colonel looked around the room before continuing. "Intel says that this man, David Alexander, aka Dawud Iskandar, former employee of the French company that manufactures the Milan, has obtained a guidance system, and is currently in his home country of Sierra Leon and will be meeting Al-Qadir in Nigeria in three days." The Colonel turned up the lights and then passed around file folders. "Your orders—"

Chapter Twenty

Now that Monk had completed his assigned task, he went to get paid. He got out of bed and got ready to go to the King's restaurant. When he got there, he was escorted to Robert's office. Ronnie was there waiting for him, seated behind his father's desk; but he wasn't alone.

Rain was still angry, so she decided to make an unannounced visit to see Ronnie. Although he was happy to see her, he knew her timing was bad, and told her that he was expecting a business associate.

"No problem, I'll leave," Rain said and started for the door, but Ronnie stopped her.

"You oughta have dinner with me tomorrow."

"You know I got a man," Rain said.

"Then what are you doing here?"

"What, a bitch can't drop by and visit an old friend?"

"A bitch can do whatever she wants, but a lady may have had a different reason," Ronnie said and touched Rain's face.

Just then, the door opened, and Monk walked into the room. "Sorry, King; didn't realize that you was busy. I could come back later."

"You don't have to go," Rain said, and stepped away from Ronnie. "I was just about to leave."

"I'll just be a minute," Ronnie said and escorted Rain to the door. "We'll continue this conversation next time."

"What conversation? I already told you I got a man, so that shit you wanna talk about ends right here."

"We'll talk about that next time I see you," Ronnie said.

Rain laughed. "If there is a next time," she whispered as she left the office.

Rain left thinking that this was a bad idea. She had gone there looking for an old friend to talk to about her and Nick. She realized that Ronnie King wasn't that person.

That nigga just want some of this pussy.

"Mr. Monk," Ronnie said and returned to his father's chair.

"King."

"Have a seat. My father will be with you in a minute."

"Thanks," Monk said and took a seat in front of the desk.

"Any problems?"

"I don't have problems."

For the next five minutes, there was silence in the office. Each man sat and looked at the other. Ronnie didn't like Monk, and more importantly, he didn't trust him. If he had his way, Ronnie would have had Monk come to his office. The drop cloth would be on the floor and he would have dropped Monk as soon as he walked in. That's what he wanted to do, but Robert was able to convince him that killing Monk may be bad for business. That they didn't need Monk's people from Cleveland coming to the city seeking vengeance. Ronnie agreed to a point, but he still wanted to put a bullet in Monk's brain, if for no other reason than to wipe that smug look off Monk's face.

"Sorry to keep you waiting, Mr. Monk," Robert said as he came in carrying a briefcase containing Monk's money.

"Not a problem. Long as you got that," Monk said and pointed to the briefcase.

Ronnie got up from behind his father's desk and let Robert sit down. "Sure you don't want me to kill him?" Ronnie whispered and Robert simply ignored him.

Robert placed the briefcase in front of Monk and sat down. He opened the case. "You may count it if you wish."

"Not necessary. I'm sure it's all there." Monk closed the case and stood up. "Pleasure doing business with you, King."

Robert nodded graciously. "What time is your flight?"

"Tomorrow afternoon," Monk said and started for the door. "Don't bother sending the limo for me. I'll find my way."

"I don't trust him, Pop," Ronnie said the second Monk closed the door.

"I think you've made that clear, Ronald. Hurry now; put somebody on him. Make sure he leaves," Robert said, and Ronnie went to carry out his father's orders.

By the time Monk got back to his hotel room, his men were getting restless. They didn't trust Monk or anybody else, for that matter. The consensus in the room was that Monk was taking too fuckin' long to get back and had probably left the city with their money.

"Knowing that nigga, he probably back in Cleveland between some woman's thighs," Mobley said as Monk opened the door and came in carrying the briefcase he got from King.

"Damn right, I'd be on some pussy," Monk said and pulled out his gun. He shoved it in Mobley's mouth. "Next time you think about accusing me of anything, I'll kill you where you stand. Got that!"

"Yes, boss."

Monk sat the case down on the bed and sat next to it. "Maybe you don't want to get paid?" he asked, and Mobley didn't answer. He knew not to fuck with Monk. Monk would kill you for the slightest sign of disrespect.

Now that everybody was paid and happy, Monk poured himself a drink and joined his men in the celebration of their good fortune. They had their money, there was plenty of drugs and alcohol for them, and they were talking about calling up some working girls. They were laughing and talking until the subject of going back to Cleveland came up.

"I don't know about y'all niggas, but I don't wanna go back to Cleveland."

"Why not?" Monk asked, even though he was thinking the same thing.

"Look, Monk," Dylan began. "I'm a stick-up kid; that's how I gets mine. Shoving my gat in a mutha fucka's face and taking his shit."

"That's the Cleveland way," Bailey said and raised his glass. Everybody in the room raised and drained his glass.

"But this shit right here; these niggas here, easy fuckin' pickings." Monk and the other men laughed. "I'm serious, Monk. This shit is paradise compared to Cleveland. These New York niggas is all rep. Ain't putting in no hard work. Paper's been good up here and I'm thinking about staying awhile longer and getting mine."

"Reason shit been so easy for us is that we had the targets handpicked and set out on a platter for us. It'd be different without that shit," Monk said.

"No, Monk, it's like that regardless. I'm telling you, these New York niggas is all rep."

"You sure about that?" Monk asked. "'Cause I know of some hustlers that run a tight program."

"Since we been here, couple of us been scouting out and hitting some of these niggas on our own."

"How'd that go?"

"Went great, Monk. Easy like the ones we did for King."

Monk looked around the room. "What about the rest of you niggas; y'all wanna stay here too?" Everybody nodded their heads. "I guess that settles that," Monk said. "We stay for a couple of days. Besides, I got something I was thinking about doing."

"That's what I'm talking about."

"This where that real paper is, nigga; trust me."

"So what you got up, Monk?"

"Yeah, anything in whatever you got for us?"

"Maybe," Monk said and got up to refresh his drink. "Like I said, I was thinking about it. I gotta do some more intel to be sure. But shit yeah."

"So what you got, Monk?"

"I went over the info we got from King and all of them had one thing in common."

"What's that?"

"They all buy from the same supplier. Guy named Nicolò De Luca; does business out of a place called Paesano on Mulberry Street."

"You gonna kill him?"

"Of course, but I got something else in mind."

For the next two days, Monk hung around Paesano and as discreetly as a black man could in Little Italy, watched Nicolò De Luca to see when to hit him. Monk quickly noted that although he hung around with a lot of people, De Luca only had one bodyguard that never left him. The thing to do was to hit him away from Paesano.

Monk decided to watch the building for a while, and then leave to find a good spot to ambush De Luca. His wait wasn't long. Monk spotted De Luca's bodyguard coming out of Paesano. He looked left and then right, before giving Nico Dees the all-clear. Monk decided not to wait.

Knowing which direction they would need to go to get to their car, Monk got out of his and headed in that direction. Along the way, he looked for a dark and secluded place to take them. Once Monk found what he considered the perfect spot, he hid in the shadows and waited for his prey.

When Nico Dees and his bodyguard were in position, Monk stepped out of the shadows. "Got a light?"

Nico stopped and his bodyguard turned around and stepped in Monk's direction. Monk kicked him in the side of his knee, and he went down to one knee. Monk quickly moved in behind the bodyguard, held his jaw and placed his hand on the back of the man's head. Then turned his head all the way in one direction, and then very swiftly jerked the head back in the opposite direction. Nicolò De Luca's bodyguard went down hard.

Monk pulled out his gun and pointed it at De Luca.

"What the fuck is this about? Do you know who the fuck I am? I'm a made fuckin' man!" he yelled.

"Whatever." Monk shot Nicolò De Luca three times in the head.

Chapter Twenty-one

Jack drove Shy's rental car to the hotel to pick her up for the day. When he arrived, naturally, she was on the phone with Black and was nowhere near ready.

"Hold on, Michael," she said and went to the door. Shy opened the door and immediately put her finger over Jack's lips. "On the phone."

Jack shook his head and walked into the room.

"I'm sorry, Michael. What were we talking about?"

"We were talking about you being my wife."

"Right. And you said that you'd be patient with me."

"I did say that."

"But you're losing patience, aren't you? You're ready to give up on me and go back to your son's mother."

"No. I will never lose patience with you. I don't want anybody else but you," he said, and thought about Jada and the things he was beginning to feel for her. He pushed those feelings to the side. "I will be right here; I don't care how long it takes." And he meant that. There was nothing that he wanted more than to be with Shy. He loved her; that never changed. All the years she was gone, no matter how much time passed, he thought of her every day.

What he had going with CeeCee was good, but it couldn't compete with his time with Shy. It was like he'd lost and CeeCee was the consolation prize.

"I don't know why you don't understand that; and honestly, Cassandra, sometimes I think you understand perfectly, but for reasons known to only you, you've decided to do this."

"Do what?"

"Don't play with me, woman," Black said.

"Yeah, but I'd like to," Shy said sweetly.

"You got a funny way of showing it."

"I know, I know. I know this hasn't been easy on you, either. But please, be patient with me just a little while longer. I've got a few things that I need to work out and I've got some things I need to take care of up here, and then we'll get together and see what happens then. But I love you, Michael. Nothing can change that."

"I love you too, Cassandra. I just want you to come home and for us to be a family again," he said, and thought about the night he came home to his family and thought he'd found her dead.

How could you not have known? was the question he asked himself since the day Monika opened the door and there she was. Alive. And looking just as she did the last time he had seen her. At first, he thought that this was some type of cruel joke that was being played on him.

How could she be alive? I saw her. Saw her dead and held her in my arms.

He had talked to Bobby about it and what he said made sense. "Look, Mike, you came home to your house and you found a woman that looked like Shy. You saw exactly what they wanted you to see. Obviously, there were people who spent a lot of time and effort putting this thing together. The woman; the police just showing up the way they did."

"Don't you think that I thought about all that? Right down to police response times in that area."

"But after a while you went on; you came to the logical conclusion and accepted it. You were in jail for murdering your wife. That's what they wanted you to believe and it worked. Don't be so hard on yourself, Mike. You're only human," Bobby told him that day. And for the most part he accepted that. But there were times when he wondered how he could not have known that woman wasn't Cassandra.

109

"Soon, I promise."

"We'll see."

"I'm gonna let you go now, Michael. I've got some things I want to get done today."

"Okay, I'll talk to you tomorrow," Black said to his wife. "I love you."

"I love you too," Shy said and ended the call.

Shy looked at Jack and shook her head. "Come home? To that house? Shiiit. It will be a cold mutha fuckin' day in mutha fuckin' hell before these two feet cross that threshold," Shy said angrily, and then she laughed a little.

It was over an hour later when Shy came out of the bathroom, but at least she was ready. Jack had fallen asleep some time ago. While he slept, Shy stood in the mirror, doing something to her head and putting on a bit of makeup. Once she was ready, she tapped Jack on the shoulder. "You ready?"

"Just waiting on you," Jack said, trying to shake it off.

"Can't get paid sleeping and talking on the phone all day."

"You a mess."

"So they tell me," Shy agreed as she walked out of the room with Jack right behind her.

For the rest of the afternoon, Shy and Jack were in the streets. Jack was anxious to show Shy the work he had put in getting things setup for them. Although she was impressed and satisfied with what he had done in so short a time, her mind was elsewhere.

This was not how she wanted things to go. Shy always imagined coming home to Black and Michelle and they would move on like the ordeal never happened. Never in her wildest dreams or nightmares could she have imagined coming home to this. *But it is what it is,* she tried to tell herself. But that was of little consolation.

What was funny was that Shy could have exactly what she wanted, anytime she wanted. She wanted to be with Black; he wanted to be with her. The only thing standing in their way was Shy and what she wanted.

I want to be wined and dined, pampered and spoiled. I want to feel loved and cared for and protected. I don't think that's too much to ask from my husband. I've been through a lot.

But that is not what I got.

So instead of island hopping with me, Michael is down there in that house, being a father to his children, which is what he's supposed to be doing. And I am so proud that I have a man, especially a man like him, that wants to be a father to his children. But I still want him with me. Selfish, right?

But honestly, this is my fault. Like it or not, I asked for this. I asked for this that first night I came back. Michael was telling me about her, and I asked the question. "Do you love her?" I asked and braced myself for the answer.

"No, I can't love her because I love you, Cassandra," he said, and I melted. That was the only answer I wanted to hear. I settled into his arms and began thinking about a happy future. But then I started thinking about the reality of the situation.

"I know that you have a relationship with this woman, and you have a child together," *I said, because it was the truth. It was what I said next that sometimes I wish I could take back.* "And I'm not gonna get in the way of that."

"So what are you saying?"

He gave me a chance to back down. I could have said anything then. I could have said that I'm not going to get in the way of you spending time with your son.

But I didn't.

I stepped right into it. "I'm saying that I'm jealous. And I have no intention of sharing you with this woman." I'm not sure if I expected him to say something gallant like, "You won't have to, because I'm yours."

But he didn't.

Then I heard myself saying, "While I was on that island, I used to hope that you were happy and had moved on with your life. Now I'm back and see that you have, and I'm ashamed to say that I'm jealous. I want to be with you; and for us to be a family again more than anything in the world."

"So do I." See, this is the part where I get confused. He's saying that he wants exactly what I want, but I still press forward with it.

"I guess in time we'll see if you really mean that." I guess I had decided then and there, what I was gonna do. I wanted to spend every minute of every day loving my man and him loving me. I wanted to go to the places we talked about going before all this madness began. I could see the pained and confused look in Michael's eyes. "I think you should go now."

"Shy!" Jack yelled to bring Shy out of the conversation she was having with herself.

"What?"

"I asked you if you heard what's been happening?"

"No. What's going on?"

"I told you that Leon killed Rico, and that left things pretty wide open. Well, Leon hasn't stepped in the top spot because he is more businessman than gangster."

"What about it?"

"What I heard was that in the last few days, some of the people that might have stepped into that void have turned up dead."

112

"Anybody I might remember?"

"You remember Bruno Franks?"

"Him I remember."

"He's dead. I think these niggas is killing each other off."

"You're probably right. That's how that game is played," she said, thinking that was never how she ran her program. "But my question is, is all that good for us or bad for us?"

"Good for us. While these niggas fight it out, it gives us a chance to build up; get some muscle."

"Hold up. What are you saying?"

"That once the smoke clears, that the last man standing will be weak from them going at each other and we'll be in a stronger position to take them on."

"I don't think that's a good idea."

"Why?"

"Because I don't wanna die, Jack. And I don't want you to die. All that shooting and killing; that's not how we did business. We stayed away from all that."

"Yeah, and look how that turned out?"

"That was because I trusted E and he betrayed us; but the program was sound. I'm not in this to take unnecessary risks with my life. I'm in this to make money." *At least that's what I keep telling myself, or is it something else?* "No, Jack. That is not the direction we need to be going in."

Jack drove on and said that he agreed with what she was saying. But the truth is that Jack had already decided that that was the direction he was going in, and had already taken steps to make it happen.

Chapter Twenty-two

With the influx of fresh capital from CeeCee, it didn't take BB long to get their operation up and running. Things weren't running smooth yet, but he assured CeeCee that he knew what he was doing, and it wouldn't take him long to get their program where it needed to be for them to get paid before he started looking to expand.

"Expand!" CeeCee all but shouted.

"Yes, CeeCee. Once I get this thing right, we gonna make a move and expand to the top." What he hadn't told CeeCee was that he didn't put all of the money that he got from her into the product. He got just enough to push his way back into the market. When he first got the money, his intention was to get as much as he could and enter the market with a low price and high quality product, but recent events had caused him to rethink that.

"I thought that was what you were gonna do with the money you got from me? You said that since Leon killed Rico, the area is wide open."

"It is."

"But now you're telling me something different."

"That's because shit's changing daily in them streets."

"How so?" CeeCee asked.

"You didn't think I was the only one who saw Leon killing Rico as an opportunity, did you?"

CeeCee didn't say anything at first, mainly because she hadn't given it any thought. Then she said. "What's going on?"

"A lotta niggas had the same idea and they been killing each other off."

"Like who?" CeeCee asked, because she hadn't heard from Blunt in a couple of days.

"Nobody you would know."

"How you know who I know?"

"My bad. I forgot you get around."

CeeCee laughed a little. "I wouldn't have put it that way. Let's just say I know a lot of people and leave it at that."

"No disrespect intended," BB said graciously.

"None taken. Now, who are we talking about?"

"We talking about Tree and his brother, Ramos. You know them?"

"No. Who else?"

"What about Tone Edmonds and B Money; you know them?" BB asked and laughed. CeeCee frowned. "Don't know them either, huh?"

"Who else?"

"I know you know Sly Stone. Everybody knows Sly."

"I do know him, and no, I am not talking about the singer."

"The other nigga that got killed was Donald Henderson; they call him Dee Mac. You ain't never heard of him either, have you?" Once again, CeeCee was silent. "Like I said, nobody you would know." BB laughed.

"Just tell me what's up,"

"Okay. With niggas killing each other off the way they are, I figured all I ..."

"You mean we, you figured all we ..."

"I figured all we had to do was sit back and wait, and be ready to move in with our product."

"Okay," CeeCee said, "that sounds reasonable. But next time, *partner*, let me know what you're doing."

"I can do that." BB got up.

"Where you going?" CeeCee asked.

"I'm about to get in them streets. See what's up with our team." CeeCee got up too. "Where you going?"

"I'm about to get in them streets. See what's up with our team," CeeCee said and grabbed her purse. "See, I think the best way for me to know what's going on is to see for myself."

"I've known you long enough to know that it's pointless to argue with you." He looked at her. "You got a gun in that purse?"

"No." CeeCee laughed a little.

"You wasn't planning on hitting them streets without your popper, were you? Wait, better question; do you actually have a popper?"

"Yes." CeeCee still had Kevon's gun that she had the night Black got shot in Freeport. "But I think it's too big a weapon for me to handle."

"Get it anyway, and I'll get you something smaller while we're in the streets," BB said. CeeCee got her gun and they left.

Their first stop was to take care of CeeCee's gun issues. BB drove to the home of a friend name David Gizzi, who dealt in weapons of all types.

"BB, what's happening? Didn't expect to see you again so soon," David said and invited them in. Then he got a good look at CeeCee. "But, dude, you could show up at my door with a pretty lady like this anytime." He took a step closer to CeeCee and bowed at the waist. "David Gizzi at your service."

"You may call me Ms. Collins."

"In fact, Davey, Ms. Collins is the reason we're here."

"Oh really."

"Yes, Mr. Gizzi," CeeCee said and sat down without being asked. David quickly sat down next to her. CeeCee crossed her legs and his eyes got big. "I was hoping you

ROY GLENN

would be able to recommend a more suitable weapon for me to carry than what I have now."

"What are you packing now, my dear?"

"May I?"

"By all means." CeeCee reached in her purse and pulled out Kevon's .45. "I see what you mean." David got up and went into another room, but returned quickly with three leather-bound cases. He handed CeeCee a set of plastic gloves. "Those are more for your protection than mine."

"I understand," CeeCee said and put them on.

"Here are my personal favorites," he said and opened the case. He took out a gun and handed it to her. "Glock Model 36. Slim and sleek. I used to carry this gun religiously. In fact, I pulled it on two miscreants who tried to approach my vehicle at an intersection."

"That's a good gun," BB commented.

"What about that one?" CeeCee pointed.

"Kel-Tec P3AT." David handed her the weapon. "The Kel-Tec P3AT is an excellent choice and I have carried it off and on over the years." David looked at CeeCee and noticed that she wasn't impressed. He had handed her another gun. "This is the Kahr PM9, it's a great little shooter; has perfect weight and balance."

CeeCee held the gun. "What about that one?" she asked and pointed to another one.

"Glock Model 19; a perfect combination of beautiful, ugly, fit and balance. It's a wonderful shooter with easily manageable recoil and excellent shot follow-up." David quickly handed her another gun. "That is the Springfield XD Compact .45. I like this gun. It's a great match of balance and power in a medium package that is extremely accurate outside the normal defensive range of seven to ten feet. Or this one," he said and handed CeeCee the gun.

117

"This is the Smith and Wesson M&P full size .40 S&W. I've owned and carried the 9mm and the .40 in both compact and full-size frames and I gotta tell yah, the reason this gun outshines other manufacturers of similar size and caliber is the grip. The interchangeable back-straps on a gun this size, for someone like me with smaller hands, makes shooting this gun a joy!"

CeeCee held the gun in her hand and pointed it. "I like that."

"Good," BB said and jumped up. "That's the one you want?" He pulled a stack of bills from his pocket.

"I would like to see what else Mr. Gizza has before I make a decision, unless you're in a hurry."

BB reclaimed his seat. "No, Cee, take your time."

"Don't call me that," she said quickly. It was what Black used to call her.

"Yeah, dude, relax, and don't rush the lady." He handed her another gun. "Glock Model 22 Gen 4. Not a small gun by any stretch; the new Gen 4 grip fits your hand perfectly. The proven stopping power of the .40 cal makes this a great choice for a full size CCW gun. Then there's the Glock Model 23. Slightly smaller than the model 22, the Glock 23 is a hands down winner in my opinion." Then he handed CeeCee a Smith and Wesson Model M&P 340 CT Revolver. "I have carried this gun for two years. This little snub-nosed revolver is the finest J-Frame ever made. Scandium alloy frame and crimson trace grips with the XS Tritium Sights makes this gun an absolute must have. Pricey ... but worth it. But my favorite is the North American Arms NAA .22 Magnum Mini-Revolver."

"What, are you serious?" BB asked.

"You bet I am. A concealed-carry handgun does you absolutely no good if it isn't carried. The NAA .22

eliminates every possible excuse you can think of for not carrying some type of personal defense gun on your person at all times. It fits all possible attire from a bathing suit to full winter garb."

CeeCee cracked a little smile. "I like the sound of that."

"No, the .22 magnum is not my favorite choice of defensive caliber, but the NAA .22 in my pocket under any possible scenario, certainly beats the hell out of my main carry gun in the glove box. In fact, this gun should be on your person even when you're carrying your main gun."

CeeCee chose, and BB paid David for the Glock 23 and the NAA .22 Magnum Mini-Revolver.

Chapter Twenty-three

After that, they hit the streets. "So let me ask you a question," CeeCee said as they drove.

"What's that?"

"You've been gone for at least a couple of years, right?"

"A little more like four; but yeah, what about it?"

"You've been back in the city for how long?"

"A month ... maybe two months."

"And it ain't been that long since I gave you this paper. So my question is; how'd you put a team together that quick?"

"How the white boys say it; this ain't my first rodeo; this is what I do," BB replied and kept driving. His answer really didn't satisfy her, but it would do for the time being. Truth was that BB got together as many street soldiers as he could as quickly as possible.

When he left the city, he went and hid out on the island with his cousin, Dex, in Wyandanch. He was dealing weed when BB got there and was more than happy to flip the product. Always having more heart than his cousin, it was Dex who encouraged BB to return to New York.

"We getting too fuckin' big to be fuckin' around out here," Dex told BB the day they talked about what was going on in the city. "Time for us to grab the reins."

At the time, they had a crew of six strong soldiers, and they brought all of them with them when they made the move. All of them stayed with Dex when they hit the streets. The rest of the team was made up of people that used to work for BB before he bounced; a couple of Cash's people, and the rest were some young bangers from around the way.

At their first stop, CeeCee was horrified to see how badly things were being run. There were no less than ten people. That was one of the spots BB had left to the bangers. "Is it always this unorganized?" CeeCee asked.

BB didn't answer; he just put the car in park and got out. CeeCee got out and leaned against the hood. "You coming?"

CeeCee shook her head. "I'm just here to observe."

"Whatever," BB said and walked off.

CeeCee watched as they hollered at every car that rolled by, whether they showed any interest in buying product or not. When a car did stop, everybody rushed the car. She shook her head as they consistently undercut one another on price. Two of them got into an argument over who was going to serve a returning customer.

"He's mine," each one shouted, and then guns were drawn. BB had to step in the middle while another banger slipped in and did business.

As they drove away from the spot, CeeCee wondered why BB allowed them to go on like that. It couldn't be good for business for them to be consistently undercutting each other on price. But being unsure of how things worked, CeeCee remained silent, and thought about baseball. She thought that if they were a team, then there should be one person designated to handle the product and the rest should divide into groups; one to handle the foot traffic and the other to handle cars.

They got to their next spot in time to watch everybody scatter as the cops rolled up on them. CeeCee thought there was somebody she could talk to about that. It would be first on her list of things to do.

The next spot was run by Cash Money's old set. They were more organized there, but it was clear that they had no respect for BB. A few of them recognized CeeCee from the old days when she used to roll with Cash. As they drove away from there, CeeCee thought that they showed her more respect than they did BB. She knew that couldn't be good for business, either. It wasn't much better at the spot run by BB's old New York crew.

"You been real quiet all night, CeeCee, what's up with that? You usually got a whole bunch to say."

"I told you; I'm just along for the ride as an observer."

"Yeah, yeah, but I know you got a mutha fuckin' opinion."

"You're right, I do. And you will hear it when I'm done," CeeCee said and looked out the window.

"Well, I do want you to say something next time we stop."

"Why?"

"I want you to meet my cousin, Dex," BB said. And it wasn't long after that when they arrived at Dex's spot. When they slowed down, one person walked slowly toward the car and turned around when they saw it was BB. *This is more like it*, CeeCee thought but didn't say.

They got out of the car and walked over to where Dex was sitting on the hood of a car. "What up, cuz?" Dex said.

"Ain't nothing," was BB's standard reply. "How things going?"

"Had a little problem with some niggas that thought this was their spot, but I crushed that."

"What you do?"

"Let's just say it's hard to sling rock when you ain't breathing no more," Dex leaned closed to BB and said. Then he turned to CeeCee. "You must be CeeCee."

"I am," CeeCee said.

"I'm Dex. It's good to finally meet you. Cuz done told me a lot about you."

"Good to meet you too."

122

"How's it going?" BB asked Dex.

Dex smiled. "I just told you; there was some niggas that thought this was they spot, but they ain't breathing no more so I don't think they gonna be a problem."

"Handle your business, boy," BB said.

Dex looked at CeeCee. He ran his tongue over his lips, smiled and stepped to her. "Come on. Let me show you how we run our program 'round here."

"Okay," CeeCee said and hoped that his program was tighter than what she had seen so far.

"You see that guy there and the one down there?"

"Yes."

"They lookouts. Their job is to make sure that we don't get caught slipping."

"By the cops?" CeeCee asked.

"Cops, rival crews, whatever or whoever might be out there to hurt us. That man there is security; but shit, the security of the team is everybody's responsibility. That right there is Lightman," Dex said and Lightman nodded. "He handles the product, and those two are runners."

"Yo, Dex," BB said, "I need to holla at you."

"Excuse me, CeeCee. That nigga always was a rude mofo," Dex said and followed BB.

While BB and Dex talked, CeeCee stood back and watched how things worked there. She was pleased to see the things at this spot were organized; not at all like the other spots they'd been to.

BB walked up to her quickly. "Come on, we out."

Dex joined them at the car. "Where you off to now?" he asked BB.

"I'ma roll by Juney."

"That nigga ... I don't know what to say about that nigga, cuz. I mean, damn, if he was your best earner back then, I don't see how you made paper." Dex shook his head. "I'm telling you now, cuz, if he don't tighten up—" Dex said and ran his thumb slowly across his throat. "Then put Lightman in that spot."

"Do you, Dex."

"All right now, you know how I do it. Won't be shit for me to measure that nigga for a body bag."

"What I just say, Dex; do you," BB said and got in the car.

Dex opened the car door for CeeCee. "I hope I see you again."

"I'm sure you will and very soon," CeeCee said and got in the car.

As they drove off, Lightman walked over and joined Dex. "That's a bad bitch there," Dex said.

"Easy, nigga. That there is Mike Black's baby mama," Lightman said.

"Ask me if I give a fuck about Mike Black," Dex said as he and Lightman got back to business.

As promised, BB's next stop was Juney's. He and Juney came up together and while The Commission was active and carrying power, Juney was BB's top lieutenant and best earner. But that was years ago. Since then, Juney had been in and out of jail and had developed a little habit along the way. This made Juney sloppy and of no use to Dex whatsoever; and at this point, BB wasn't far from sharing Dex's opinion.

When they got to the spot, BB didn't like what he saw. He opened his door and then turned to CeeCee. "Wait here."

CeeCee looked on as BB rushed up to somebody she assumed was Juney. She could tell by their body language that they were having a very intense argument. As the argument raged on, CeeCee sat and wondered if she had gambled her money on the wrong horse. With the exception of Dex and Lightman, every spot they went to seemed in total disarray to her.

When Juney turned his back, BB walked away and took out his cell phone. He got in the car. "Yo, Dex. This B, man. That thing we was just talking about, go on and make that happen," BB said and hung up. "I need to take you home, baby doll."

"Okay," CeeCee said quietly. She knew that BB had just sanctioned Juney's murder and wondered if, in her position, if that made her an accessory. If she was going to do this, it was time for her to take a more active role.

Chapter Twenty-four

Oasis on Park is located at 1 Park Avenue, in the heart of Manhattan, between East 32nd and East 33rd Streets. Oasis on Park features 19 treatment rooms including saunas, and also features a hair and nail salon.

The day before, Jada took her mother shopping for a new wardrobe; today was spa day. When the phone rang in their suite, Jada answered. "Good morning."

"Good morning, Ms. West. This is Duke speaking. I just wanted to let you know that I am parked outside."

"Excellent."

"Do you need me to come up and get you, Ms. West?"

"I don't think that will be necessary. I'm sure we can find our way."

"As you wish, Ms. West," Duke said.

"We'll be down in ten minutes," Jada said as her mother came out of her room, wearing the nightgown and robe Jada had bought her the day before. Her hair was tied with a scarf, and a cigarette was dangling from her lip. "Better make that an hour, Duke. I will call you before we come down."

"As you wish, Ms. West," Duke said, and Jada ended the call.

"Good morning, Mommy."

"Hey, baby girl. What's gonna be more like an hour?"

"You said that you had never been to a spa, so I made an appointment for us to go to the spa today."

Vivian laughed, and then she came and sat down next to her daughter. "I'll let you in on a little secret."

"What's that, Mommy?"

"I don't know what a spa is." Jada laughed. "So why don't you start out by telling me what a spa is, okay?"

"Okay," Jada paused and thought for a minute. "The spa we're going to offers different types of massages, manicure and pedicure, and a variety of facials to choose from. They offer rejuvenating hand treatments, scalp treatments, and a body scrub and wrap combo."

"Body scrub and wrap combo? What's that?"

"A body scrub and body wrap combo eliminates dead skin and clears the pores. The body wrap penetrates deep into the skin removing toxins from clogged pores all over the body."

"Oh," Vivian said, still unsure what that meant.

"So why don't you go ahead and get ready, so we are not too late for our appointment."

"Okay," Vivian said and got up, but she was less than enthusiastic about going.

As she got ready, she thought about the day they had yesterday. They shopped just about the entire day, had lunch and dinner, and topped off the evening with drinks at Salon De Ning, the rooftop bar at the Peninsula Hotel. They did everything except talk, which seemed like the one thing Jada didn't want to do.

Once Vivian was ready, she came out of the room. Jada sprung to her feet and picked up the phone. "Yes, Ms. West."

"We are on our way."

"I will be ready when you get here," Duke said.

"Thank you," Jada said and started moving toward the door.

Vivian followed her out. "I was hoping that we'd have some time for us to talk."

"There is plenty of time for that, Mother." Jada stopped, turned around, and faced Vivian. "Unless, of course, you're planning on going back to jail."

"Oh, hell no!" Vivian shouted. "With God as my witness, this bitch ain't ever going back there."

"Well then, we've got all the time in the world," Jada said. As she approached the limo, Duke got out and opened the door for her. The ladies got in and Duke closed the door.

"I'm serious, Jada. There are some things I want to talk to you about."

"I know, Mommy, and I promise we will; but for right now, can't you just relax and let me pamper you?"

"Okay, baby girl. I can do that."

Duke got in the limo. "Where to, Ms. West?"

"Oasis on Park, Duke. It's located at 1 Park Avenue, between East 32nd and East 33rd Streets," Jada said. And a short time later she and Vivian were being greeted by the staff at Oasis on Park.

"Welcome back, Ms. West. It has been so long since your last visit with us. And who is this lovely lady?"

"Giorgio, this is my mother, Mrs. West."

"Mother," Giorgio said and looked horrified. "This cannot be your mother ... older sister maybe."

Vivian laughed a bit. But since she knew it was just a line that he had probably run a thousand times, she didn't make too much of it. "It's true. I am her mother."

"And this is her first time at a spa, so I was thinking that we would start out with a massage," Jada said.

"Excellent idea, Ms. West. Our signature massage uses long strokes and light to medium pressure to improve circulation and diminish stress. Perfect for first-timers."

"That's me; virgin first-timer."

"Do you know what type of massage you want?"

Jada looked at her mother and then back to Giorgio. "Why don't you explain some of our choices?"

"You can choose the For Your Way massage, which gives you 30 minutes for you to specify your troubled areas. Tell the therapist where you want them to focus. Our Deep Tissue massage uses slow strokes and firm pressure. It helps relieve chronic pain and increase range of motion. Our Muscle Meltdown massage melts away your aches and pains. It's a massage that combines moist heat, Biofreeze, and cool marble stones. We also offer a Lava Stone massage, Aromatherapy massage, and of course, our Swedish massage that uses specially blended oil to soothe the mind, body and spirit. You can choose from our selection of aromatherapy oils to suit your mood."

"So much to choose from," Vivian giggled and looked at Jada.

"We'll start out with a Side-by-Side Swedish massage."

"Excellent choice! Right this way, ladies," Giorgio said and led them to one of their side-by-side treatment rooms.

Before the day was done, Jada and Vivian had experienced and enjoyed an Oasis Signature facial that was individually customized for their skin types, which included skin analysis, exfoliation and extractions to stimulate cell renewal for a healthy complexion; an Oasis Signature scalp treatment; a luxurious scalp massage using warm Moroccan oils to calm and relax the body, while nourishing and balancing dry, oily skin and hair.

Then they had the revitalizing eye treatment, which was a gentle exfoliation designed to reduce the appearance of fine lines, with a cool stone massage to relax facial tension and stimulate circulation to help reduce dark circles and de-puff stressed eyes.

"I really needed that," Vivian said as she looked in the mirror. "I can see a big difference."

They ended spa day with a rejuvenating hand treatment, followed by a Citrus Brown Sugar Scrub and a Body Hydrating Wrap.

Then it was off to Aquagrill on Spring Street and Sixth Avenue, where they dined on appetizers, which included a chunky Maine lobster salad, a spicy tuna tartare, and fresh Atlantic and Pacific coast oysters.

After appetizers, executive chef-owner Jeremy Marshall came around to their table. "My specialty is grilled Atlantic salmon with a falafel crust and plump seared sea scallops with crab meat polenta," he explained.

"Sounds tasty," Jada said and giggled a bit.

"The kitchen's version of bouillabaisse is among the best this side of Paris. If you don't appreciate exotic preparations or you're on a diet, which neither of you need to be, you can order just about anything grilled, poached or roasted. Our desserts are rich and frivolous, and the wine list is long on fish-friendly varieties."

At the completion of what really was an excellent meal, they returned to the Peninsula hotel. "Will you need me for anything else this evening, Ms. West?" Duke asked as he escorted them to the door.

"I don't think so, Duke. And I will call you in the morning and let you know my plans for the day."

"As you wish, Ms. West."

As Jada and Vivian walked through the lobby toward the elevator, Jada leaned close to her mother. "I could really get used to having Duke around."

"He is a real cutie," Vivian said, and Jada looked horrified.

"I wasn't referring to that. I was talking about how polite and efficient he is," Jada said and paused. "But, yeah, he is a real cutie."

"Why you look at me like I'm not supposed to notice a good-looking man?"

"I don't know; maybe because you're my mother."

"Whatever, girl."

"Did you want to stop at the bar and get a drink?" Jada asked.

"No. If I want another drink, I can get it out of the mini bar in the room. Right now, I just want to relax," Vivian said and looked at her daughter. Jada knew what that meant, and she wasn't looking forward to it.

Vivian wanted to talk.

When they got to the room, as promised, Vivian went straight to the mini bar, grabbed two bottles of Bacardi, a glass and some coke, and made herself a drink. She took a sip.

"You want me to make you a drink, baby girl?" she said to nobody. She turned around and looked around the room. "Jada?" But Jada had slipped quietly into her room.

Vivian laughed, lit up a cigarette, and sat down with her drink. She waited until she heard the sound of the shower running, then she got up, drink in hand, and slipped quietly into Jada's room and sat down on the bed.

A few minutes later, Jada came out of the bathroom and was surprised to see her mother sitting there. "What are you doing?"

"You and I are gonna talk and we are gonna talk now," Vivian said in a tone of voice that Jada hadn't heard since she was a little girl. "Now, you sit your fat ass down and talk to me."

"My ass is not fat," Jada insisted.

"Shiiit! Big fat ass, baby girl. You got the kind of ass that makes men follow you around."

"Sounds like somebody is jealous," Jada said and walked out of the room.

"Damn right, I'm jealous. I used to be a bad bitch back in the day," Vivian said and followed Jada out of the room.

"Well, I guess the bad bitch apple don't fall far from the bad bitch tree," Jada said as she walked.

"And where do you think you're going?"

"I'm just going to get a drink, Mommy." Vivian sat down and lit another cigarette while Jada made herself a drink. "And you were, too," Jada said as she poured. "There wasn't anybody fine like my mommy." Jada turned around. "You're still a very pretty woman. You just haven't been taking proper care of yourself lately."

Vivian laughed. "Well, there's a reason for that. I been ... you know ... away for a while."

"Do we really need to have this conversation, Mommy? I mean, you and I both know where you were. Well, you're out now. I don't understand why we can't just close that door and move forward."

"Because we have to, Jada; that's why. We need to talk about it."

"I needed to talk ten years ago, and you shut me out of your life completely."

"I couldn't deal with it then."

"I understand that now, Mommy, I really do. But back then I had just celebrated my eighteenth birthday, my daddy was dead, and they took you away in handcuffs. All I knew was that I was alone, broke, and you didn't want anything to do with me. All you left me was a seventy-seven Monte Carlo."

"That bitch was beat down, but it ran like a champ, didn't it," Vivian said.

Jada looked at her mother, took a sip, and laughed. "It was one hell of a car; but the point is still the same, Mommy. I had barely graduated from high school, so college wasn't in my future."

"Looks like you turned out damn good for somebody who barely graduated high school. Which brings me to the other question you've been avoiding since you got here, Jada."

"What's that?"

"What do you do that you can ride around with sexy-ass Duke all day? And if you haven't spent ten thousand dollars, you haven't spent a dime."

"Actually, it's closer to fifteen."

"Okay, fifteen. But the point is still the same."

"My business partner, Mr. Black, arranged for Duke and his services. He likes to make sure that I'm safe."

"What business is that?"

Jada frowned and shook her head. "Look, Mommy, when you cut me off, I had to do what I had to do to survive."

"I taught you that."

"I remember you said so many times; a woman gotta step up. Sometimes a woman gotta use what she got to get what she gotta get to take care of her family. Well, I was a family of one." Jada took a sip of her drink. "You know, sometimes I wonder how much those words and your choices, affected me and the choices I've made in life."

Vivian started laughing. "Your ass done sold some of that pussy, ain't you?"

Jada put down her glass and faced her mother. "Mother, I've shaken this ass at a strip club and sold more than some of this pussy. Now, my partner and I run an exclusive establishment in Nassau."

"What kind of establishment?"

"I am the madam of a very high-price ho house, and my partner, Mike Black, runs the gambling."

"You talking about Vicious Black?"

"He doesn't like to be called that, but that's him."

"I remember him. He's a real cutie too."

"Yeah, he said that he knew Daddy."

"Your daddy was a bad man with a stick in his hand. A legend."

There was silence in the room as both women remembered the man that, in different ways, meant so much to both of them. Vivian got up and made herself another drink.

"I'm sorry I wasn't there for you, baby girl. I wish I could say or do something to make it up to you. All I can do is say I'm sorry and hope that you find it in your heart to forgive me."

"Like I said, Mommy; I don't understand why we can't just close that door and move forward?"

"We can," Vivian said, and the two teary-eyed women hugged each other. "What we gonna do tomorrow?" she asked and quickly wiped away her tears.

"I have a business to run; so unless you have something better to do, we are leaving for Nassau in the morning."

Chapter Twenty-five

It was early in the morning when Detectives Kirkland and Bautista arrived at the crime scene. When they walked in the apartment they were met by Lieutenant Gene Sanchez from the narcotics division.

"There they are," Sanchez said and walked away from the uniformed officers he was talking to. "Good morning, Detective Bautista. ¿Cómo está usted en esta hermosa mañana?"

"Estoy muy bien, Lieutenant. Gracias por preguntar," Bautista replied.

"¿Cómo te esta tratando el tipo?" Sanchez asked and pointed at Kirk. "Le esta tratando."

"He's treating her fine," Kirk said, and both Sanchez and Bautista looked at him. "Now can we get to work here?"

"What you got for us this morning?" Bautista asked.

"Four black males murdered. From the looks of it, they were on their knees when they were shot," Sanchez informed them. "ME's been here and gone. The lab guys saved the bodies for you."

"What do you think, Bautista?" Kirk asked.

Bautista put on her gloves and crouched down next to one of the bodies. "Execution style." His hands were tied behind his back. "They've all been shot point-blank in the back of the head." Kirk looked over the other bodies and then signaled to the techs that it was all right to take the body.

Bautista nodded her head and began looking over the rest of the crime scene. "There are definitely signs of forced entry," she said as she looked at the doorframe.

Kirk walked over and joined her. "Think they kicked it in?"

Bautista rolled her eyes. "Judging from the splintering of the frame around the lock, I'd say that's a safe assumption." She didn't like being asked simple questions like that, but she was getting used to it. No matter how long she had been on the force, as far as Kirk was concerned, she was still a wet-behind-the-ears rookie. The fact that she came over from robbery-homicide meant nothing to him. Detective Bautista understood that she would have to prove herself to her new partner and she was anxious to do so.

It was like a dream come true for her to be working with him. The fact that she thought he was sexy was just the icing on the cake.

"What else, Detective?" Kirk asked as Sanchez looked on with a big smile on his face. He thought that Detective Marita Bautista was hot.

"Judging by the bullet holes in this wall, somebody shot at them. Shooter fired back." Bautista knelt down and picked up a few shells. "Doesn't seem like the firefight lasted very long."

"Reason?" Kirk asked.

"Superior firepower would be my guess, Detective."

"You got anything on those guys?" Kirk asked and pointed to where the bodies were found.

"No ID on any of them," Sanchez said. "But you know how that goes, Kirk. Wipe away a set of these scumbags and a fresh set of scumbags take their place," Sanchez said and looked at Bautista. "Dispense mi idioma."

Bautista laughed a little. "Es bueno, Detective, I've heard much worse than that."

Kirk shook his head. "Anybody canvas the building?" he asked.

"Uniforms."

"And?"

ROY GLENN

"Nobody saw anything; nobody heard anything," Sanchez said.

"Since Rico took two to the head, who's the big player in the game these days?" Kirk asked.

"That's just the thing. Nobody's stepped up to that spot yet," Sanchez said. "I think this is just the tip of the iceberg."

"So you think that these clowns are killing each other off?" Bautista asked.

Sanchez started to answer, but Kirk cut him off quickly. "If that is the case, Detective, and I'm not saying that it is, what should our next move be?"

"I think we should take a step back to gain some perspective on the case. Look at the big picture."

"And what does that fresh perspective tell you?"

"That we need to see who's sitting out the party and who has the most to gain from these assholes slaughtering each other."

Sanchez leaned closer to Kirk. "Not bad," he whispered.

Kirk didn't say anything in response and just walked toward the door. "Coming, detective?"

"Right behind you, Detective," Bautista said and followed Kirk out the door. "Lieutenant."

Sanchez bowed slightly. "Detective."

Bautista had to pick up her pace a bit to catch up with Kirk. "Where to now?" she asked.

"To follow a hunch," Kirk said as they left the building and got in his car. "Something you said about finding who's sitting out the party and who has the most to gain from these assholes slaughtering each other."

"Anybody in particular come to mind?"

"You ever heard of Robert King?"

"Can't say I have."

"Well, before we go by there, let's get you up to speed," Kirk said and headed for the precinct.

"Sounds good," Bautista said. She settled into her seat and looked at Kirk while he drove. "I didn't know you spoke Spanish, Detective."

"I don't; but if you work these streets as long as I have you learn to understand it. You know, pick up a word, a phrase here and there."

Bautista turned away and glanced out the window. "Maybe I'll teach you how to speak it," she said flirtatiously. "I'm not saying that you'll be fluent or anything like that, but you'll be able to communicate. Never know when it may come in handy."

Kirk picked up on the tone of Bautista's suggestion. "You never know," he said, and chose to keep it professional. He thought about the last time he dated another cop. Kirk ended up marrying her ... his third marriage. It lasted eight months before they were divorced. Now when they get together it's just for sex.

Once they got back to the precinct, Kirk brought Bautista all the files they had on Robert and his son, Ronnie King. For the next hour, Bautista reviewed the files the police had on them both. While they were there, Kirk was informed that they had identified that morning's body count. "Their names are Albert Blanchard," the uniform said as he handed Kirk their files, "Lewis Napier, David Frederickson and Matthew Barnett aka Matty Bump."

They took a break to go and see the ME to see if he had anything they could use. "Sorry, Kirk. Nothing spectacular about these guys."

"Thanks, Jim. Maybe the tech boys will turn up something we can use," he said, and Bautista followed him out of the lab so she could finish reviewing files.

When Kirk was satisfied that his partner was ready, they headed for the restaurant owned by the King family. When they arrived at the Kings' place, the restaurant was crowded with lunch customers.

"Smells good," Bautista said to her partner as they entered.

"Yeah, a lot of these guys who try to show a legit front, open restaurants. They tell me this is one of the better ones. They've been open for years."

"From what I read, this guy could probably go legit and make a living."

"One thing prevents that, Detective."

"What's that?"

"They're all greedy fucks who try to make all the money. King is just better at it than most," Kirk said as they approached the hostess.

"Two?" she asked.

"No," Bautista said and flashed her badge. "We're here to see Robert King."

The hostess rolled her eyes. "Follow me, please."

Kirk and Bautista looked at each other and then followed the hostess as she led them through the restaurant to the offices in the back. "I'll let Mr. King know that you're here. Someone will be with you soon," she said and walked off.

When she left, Ronnie King approached them. "Detective Kirkland, isn't it?"

"That's right. And this is my partner, Detective Bautista," Kirk said, and she showed Ronnie her badge.

"What can I do for you, detectives?" Ronnie asked.

"Just wanted to ask your father some questions."

Ronnie flashed a smile. "What would those questions be pertaining to?"

Kirk didn't seem to be amused by Ronnie's attitude. Kirk got in his face. "Let's not fuck around, kid. If you know me, then you know what I do," he said. "We're investigating several drug murders."

"Right this way," Ronnie said and opened the door to his father's office. "Excuse me, Pop, but these detectives want a word with you."

"Kirk? That you, Kirk?" Robert said more than asked. "Have a seat and tell me what I can do for you?"

"We're investigating several drug murders."

"I know it's been a minute since I've had any dealings with you, Kirk, but I gave up that game awhile back," Robert said, and Ronnie came and stood by him. "I'm afraid you and the lovely lady have wasted your time."

"Yeah, I hear you're a legitimate businessman now. But you know, guys like you, guys that have been around for a while, you never really get out; you always know what's going on. It's in the blood."

"Is that a fact?" Robert asked.

"In fact, it is."

"Since I know for a fact that you haven't heard anything about me being involved in any drug murders, tell me what you have heard, and I'll see if I can help you, Detective."

"Lately, some midlevel clowns have been getting themselves killed trying to step into some big shoes. And since they're the size shoe that once fit you perfectly, I decided I'd drop by to see if they'd still fit."

"I hope you see that even though those shoes might have fit back in the day that those days are behind me. I'm running a legitimate business here, Detective."

"Right." Kirk stood up and Bautista sprang to her feet. "You know what I'm looking for, King, so if you hear anything, I know that I'll hear from you." Kirk and Bautista headed for the door. "By the way, I never waste my time," Kirk said and left.

Robert looked at Ronnie. "You think he knows anything?" Ronnie asked his father.

"Kirk is smart. Don't underestimate him."

When the detectives got in their car and drove away, Bautista turned to Kirk. "What do you think?"

"I think a program of eliminate-and-consolidate is just the kind of thing that Robert King would come up with. But he's much too smart to get his hands, or his sons for that matter, dirty. So he's got to have somebody doing the heavy lifting. Let's find out if I'm right."

Chapter Twenty-six

It was 9 o'clock in the morning and Jack woke up wondering who was blowing up his phone at that hour of the morning. The first time he ignored it; now, not only was it ringing again, he had a new text. He looked at the display and saw it was Deacon, who was stepping up to be Jack's top lieutenant, calling.

"What you want, Deacon?"

"Sorry to bother you at this hour of the morning, but I thought you'd want to hear this right away."

"Stop fuckin' around and tell me."

"Matty Bump and three of his peeps is dead. They hit him and took the product," Deacon said.

"When this happen?" Jack asked and rolled out of bed.

"Some time last night."

"How you hear about it?"

"He was supposed to get with me last night. Said he had some shit going on that he needed to kick with me. When I didn't hear from him, I sent a couple of my boyz around to check on him; said the cops was there when they got there."

"Shit!" Jack said and glanced at the clock. "And you got no idea what he wanted to kick it about?"

"What you want me to do?"

"Nothing. I'll take care of it," he said and ended the call.

Jack got up and started to pick up the phone, but thought better of it. He knew that he needed to have all the facts before he called Shy and told her about what happened. It was a call he wasn't looking forward to making because he knew that she wasn't going to be happy.

Not just because some of their people were dead, that was bad enough, but Jack knew the reason they were dead was because he had defied Shy's orders. He had sent Matty

Bump and another one of his people, Ingram to push their way in and open new markets. He needed to find out what happened with Matty, and then he needed to make sure that Ingram hadn't suffered the same fate.

It took a while to find out just what happened. Matty Bump and his set were robbed and murdered execution style. Then it took a while longer to find out what the deal was with Ingram. He wasn't robbed and executed like the others. Ingram got into a beef over territory with some guy named Dex; but he was dead too. Now there was only one thing left to do; talk to Shy. That was a task he wasn't looking forward to.

That afternoon, Shy was doing the same thing that she did every afternoon. She was on the phone talking to Black. Now that Jack was set up, she didn't have to rush Black off the phone the way she had been. The rest of her day was spent shopping for new clothes and getting caught up with old friends. In the evening, she would call in time to say good night to Michelle, and they would talk until Black went out for the night.

As for Black, he, too, had no reason to rush her off the phone. Since Jada was in New York visiting with her mother, his afternoons were free. He hadn't heard from Jada since she'd left, but he really hadn't expected her to call every day the way Shy did. It wasn't her style. He knew she'd be back in a day or two, and he would hear from her then. Late at night, he would roll by The Grill and then Paraíso to make sure things were running smoothly.

"So what are you guys doing today?" Shy asked.

"We're out on the boat."

"You have a boat now? I'll bet it's a yacht."

"No, it's not a yacht, but it is a good size boat; and it's not exactly mine. I used to rent it out when I wanted to go out on the water. One day Oscar, that's the ship's captain, he came to me and said that times were slow. You know, with the recession and all. He couldn't afford to pay his dock fees and asked if he could dock the boat at the house."

"The house has a dock?"

"One hundred fifty-two feet on the canal."

"Oh," Shy said and rolled her eyes. She had come to hate that house and everything that it represented to her.

Black chose not to comment on her tone and continued. "The next time I was out on the boat, Oscar was telling me that his wife was having another baby and if things didn't pick up soon, he might have to sell the boat. Then he said that I was his best customer and maybe I should just pay him a salary and the boat would be at my disposal. It seemed like a good idea, so now I have a boat at my disposal."

"That's nice," Shy said and thought about the years she'd missed out on and the lifestyle that could have been hers.

"Michelle likes it."

"What's she doing? I'm surprised that she's not in your lap asking a million questions."

"She's fishing."

"Michelle is fishing? You hate to fish, Michael, how did she get into that?"

"If I told you, you'd just get mad," Black said and braced himself.

"Then don't tell me. She ever catch anything?"

"She's gotten a fish on her line and somebody is always around to reel it in for her."

"So who's with her now?"

"M is with her."

"Don't tell me M is into fishing now too?"

"No, M is more tolerant of the whole fishing thing than I am, so she doesn't mind sitting with her with a line in the water. But usually it's Oscar. When Bobby is down here he fishes with her."

"How often does Bobby get down there?"

"Now that I have the boat, Bobby is down here just about every other weekend."

"Where's Easy? Don't tell me he's fishing too?" Shy asked and hoped he'd say no.

"He's taking a nap. He takes after me; not into the fishing thing."

"I knew I liked that boy."

"So, what's been up with you?"

"You'll never guess who I had dinner with last night," Shy said, glad to be changing the subject. She hated that she was so jealous, but it was how she felt. But it made her feel good that she could have it all anytime she was ready. She just wondered why she wasn't.

"Who?"

"Porsche."

"Your sister Porsche?"

"The same."

"What's Porsche into these days?"

"Same as always; getting men to give her money," Shy said of her half-sister.

"Same old Porsche. I hear Jack is out."

"Who?" Shy said and her eyes popped opened.

"Jack, your old partner, Jack. I hear he's out now."

"We hung out a few times."

"What's he into?"

"Same as me; trying to figure out what he wants to do."

"As long as he doesn't want to sling dope, you could send him to see Bobby or Nick. They could always use a good man. And if he wants to go legit, send him to see Wanda. They'll take care of him."

"Thanks. I'll let him know. I'm surprised you haven't asked me what I'm gonna do lately."

"What's the point?"

"Excuse me?"

"No point in asking you. You'll tell me what you want to do when you're ready," Black said and hoped that she'd say that she was ready to come back to him. It was all he really wanted.

"Thank you. I appreciate that."

"No problem." There was a moment or two of silence, and then a fair amount of idle chit-chat between them as each thought about the life they could or would have when they were back together. Then there was a knock at her room door.

"Excuse me, Michael. Somebody is at my door."

"You expecting somebody?"

"No. But let me see who it is. Hold on; I'll be right back," Shy said and laid the phone down while she went to see who it was. Shy looked and saw that it was Jack. She opened the door.

"What's up, Shy?" he said, and Shy immediately put her finger over his lips.

"Shhh, I'm on the phone with Black," she said and went back to the phone.

"So what else is new," Jack said and made himself comfortable.

"Michael, that's my girlfriend Darlene," Shy lied again.

She didn't enjoy lying to him, but what else could she do. Admit that she had gotten back in the game.

Not.

"Let me see what she's talking about, okay?"

"Cool."

"I'll call you tonight to say good night to the children." Shy paused. "I love you," she said and ended the call.

When Shy came into the room Jack took a deep breath. "There is something I need to make you aware of," Jack said, and Shy stopped in her tracks.

Chapter Twenty-seven

"I don't like where this is going already," she said and sat down across from him. "Go ahead. Let's hear it."

Shy sat quietly and listened as Jack told her about Matty Bump and Ingram, and how each met their demise. He was surprised that she didn't ask any questions while he ran down all the information he was able to find out.

"Anything else?" Shy finally said.

"No, that's all of it," Jack said and waited for the type of outburst that he was accustomed to coming from Shy.

"You know what's funny?"

"What's that?"

"Well, it ain't nothing to laugh about because, what, eight or nine people are dead," Shy stood up. "But what I find interesting is that with the exception of Tony and E, we only lost one person the entire time we used to run our program."

"It's a new day."

"No, Jack, there's more to it than that. Yes, of course, it is a new day, but there is more to it than that. See, I believe, and believe me I've spent a lot of time alone thinking about this, but I truly believe that what made our program successful and relatively non-violent for as long as it was, was the fact that we weren't greedy. We understood our market and conducted ourselves accordingly. The only reason we took any losses was because there was a thief and a murderer operating inside our house. You know what I'm saying? E being who he was and doing what he did, led to Janet getting shot in the back and Tony getting killed by E's fake police. Had we sniffed out E and put a stop to what he was doing, you wouldn't have gone to jail. Shit, chances are that I may never even have met Michael. What I'm trying to say is that we knew our limitations. We didn't try to get too big too fast. If we saw an opportunity to expand we made the move, but it was done slowly and carefully." Shy paused. "Now, I know I said a lot just to ask this simple question, but is that the case here?"

"No, Shy, we are in this position because I tried to push a little harder and expand before the opportunity presented itself."

"So, what you're saying is that despite what I said about not getting involved in trying to fill the so-called void left when Leon killed Rico, that you got involved in trying to fill the void. Am I correct?"

"Yes, Shy."

"And because of that nine people are dead. What were you thinking? It's a rhetorical question; I already know the answer. You saw the brass ring and tried to grab it."

"You're right."

"So what do we do now?" Shy asked and then she said, "Hold up. The better question is; have you learned anything from your actions, which as a consequence, nine people are dead?"

"Yes, Shy," Jack said and felt like a bad child who had just been chastised by his mother. "I will work within the boundaries of our limitations, and attempt growth only when opportunity presents itself. And even then, we take our time."

"Good. So what do we do now?"

"I'm meeting with Nico Dees' people later tonight to refresh the product." Seeing the look on Shy's face, Jack quickly said, "Not that we took that heavy a loss last night, it's just time to make that move."

"Well, in light of what happened last night, I think I'm going to go with you. What time are you meeting them?"

"Ten o'clock," Jack said knowing that it was pointless to argue with her. When Shy made up her mind that she was going to do something, there was no turning her around.

"Then you have plenty of time to take me to dinner." Shy glanced at her watch. "I'll be ready soon," she said and went in her room, slamming the door behind her.

"That wasn't so bad," Jack said softly.

"I heard that," Shy yelled from the next room.

It was an hour and a half later when she came out of the room. Jack stood up and looked at his watch. It was just after seven. Plenty of time for dinner. "I hope you're taking me someplace nice," Shy said.

"You wanna grab something here in the hotel?" Jack asked.

Since she was staying in a suite at the Radisson on Lexington and 48th Street, there were a number of fine choices to choose from. There was a Chinese cuisine restaurant called Dynasty, offering a marvelous menu reflecting a respect for Chinese culinary traditions; and the Mamajuana Café, a premier Dominican colonial style café, deeply rooted in traditions dating back centuries brought back to life for the 21st century diner. In addition to the trendy Lex Lounge and Sushi Bar and a charming coffee shop named Raffles, there was a Starbucks, naturally. The hotel even hosted the Latin Quarter Nightclub, which featured live salsa music from the Mambo Kings, with sounds of Johnny Pacheco and Eddie Palmieri.

"No," Shy said. "I've eaten everywhere in the hotel."

"What do you have a taste for?" Jack asked.

"I'm feeling Italian and musical."

After a bit of discussion they settled on the Avra Restaurant; a Mediterranean Greek restaurant, which wasn't too far from the hotel between 3rd and Lexington Avenues.

Jack had the Garides Psites; simply grilled Gulf Ocean garden shrimp infused with fresh garlic and herbed olive oil, while the always adventurous Shy tried the Avra Octapodi; a grilled sushi-tender Portuguese octopus with onions and red wine vinegar. Jack passed on dessert while Shy had the Avra's Molten Chocolate Cake with Fig ice cream. After finishing what she considered a very enjoyable meal, Shy looked at her watch. "About time for us to go, ain't it?"

"Our ride should be outside now," Jack said and signaled for the check.

"Where're we meeting them?" Shy asked.

"Uptown. Spot on Burnside Avenue by Jerome," Jack replied and paid the check.

"Last time you met them at a spot in Mount Vernon. Why the change? Your idea?"

"No, this is the spot they chose. Nico's man didn't say why the change," Jack said, and Shy followed him out of Avra. They stepped out of the restaurant and a midnight blue Escalade pulled up in front of them. The passenger door swung open. "What's up, Jack?" the man said and held the door open for Shy to get in. He and Jack got in back and they drove off.

"Shy, that is Sean behind the wheel and this Nate Bounce and Walter Bogart. Fellows this is Shy."

"Good to meet you," they all said sort of in unison. "Jack talks a lot about you," Sean said as he drove. "He just never said you was this fine."

"But I do remember saying that she is Mrs. Mike Black and he will kill you for noticing, didn't I?" Jack said and tapped him in the back of the head.

"It's cool, Sean. As long as you show me and treat me with respect, we won't have any problems," Shy said.

"And that goes for you two niggas," Jack said to Nate and Bogart.

Jack handed Shy a gun. She checked it and settled into her seat for the ride uptown. While Sean drove, she thought back to the old days when she controlled every aspect of the buy, *and everything else for that matter.* She wondered if things ran better that way, or if she was just a control freak those days. For a minute, she considered taking a more hands-on approach, but then she remembered that she was just an investor/consultant in this venture. But she didn't like it. There she was, riding to a drug deal at a spot she knew nothing about, with three people she didn't know. Shy tried to relax and hoped everything would go smoothly.

It was just before ten when they arrived at the meeting place on Burnside Avenue. Even though it wasn't that late, there were very few people on the street; a few heading up the steps to catch the number 4 train.

"Drive around the block again, Sean," Shy ordered.

"You got it."

"Anybody check this place out?" Shy asked.

"I rode by here this afternoon," Sean said.

"Any other exits or is this one-way in and out?"

"I didn't get out of the car to see. There may be a back door, but I can't say for sure."

Shy looked back at Jack. "So, we're walking up in here blind? Is that what you niggas are telling me?" she asked.

Complete silence was the response she got. She wanted to tell Jack that he should know better, but she didn't want to take him to school in front of his people. But once the deal was done, Shy knew that Jack would get an earful from her. In her world, the world she used to run, procedure was everything.

"I'll take that as a yes," Shy said as they returned to the front of the building. She checked her weapon again. "Let's go."

Sean parked in front of the building and everybody got out. Shy turned back and looked at Sean. "You stay here. Keep the car running. If you see, hear, or anything goes down out here, you lean on the horn," Shy said now fully in command of the operation.

When they stepped inside, there were three black men instead of the Italians she was expecting to see. After Monk killed Nico Dees, it was his men who were setting up, robbing, and murdering dealers.

"Who are these niggas?" Shy asked.

"I never saw them before," Jack replied.

"I got a bad feeling about this," Shy said.

Meanwhile, outside at the Escalade, Bailey walked up to Sean and knocked hard on the window. Sean put his hand on his gun and rolled the window down enough to hear him. "What?" Sean asked.

"Nothing," Bailey said and shot Sean twice in the head. He opened the door, pushed Sean's body over, got in, and drove off.

Back inside, the tension was building. "Where's Nico Dees?" Jack shouted and Shy started backing up.

"He couldn't make it, so he sent us," Mobley said, and he and Dylan pulled out Norinco 86S's, a Chinese made weapon, which fired 7.62 millimeter shells from a 30-round box magazine, and opened fire, hitting Nate Bounce with their first shots.

"Not again," Shy said as she pulled her weapon and ran for cover behind some tables. Jack wasn't far behind. He turned over a table and fired back.

Shy returned fire and quickly dropped back behind the table thinking that if she could make it to the door, she might be able to get out of this. She looked the other way and saw that Bogart was pinned down not far from the door. Shy fired at Monk and his men.

Bogart made a run for the door firing as he ran, until one of his guns was empty and he went down right next to Shy. While Jack got a shot off in the direction of Monk and his men, Shy looked at the dead body lying next to her, but understood that this wasn't the time to get shaky. She took the gun out of Bogart's hand.

Shy checked the clip. It still had five shells in it. She pushed the clip back in. "We gotta make a run for that door!" Shy yelled at Jack.

Suddenly the shooting seemed to let up, as Mobley and Dylan stopped to reload their Norinco 86S's with another 30-round box magazine. Noticing that it was just Monk shooting, and he only had a handgun, Shy and Jack both jumped up firing and made their run for the door, just as the Norinco 86S's opened up.

Shy ran behind Jack, firing with both guns. As they made it out the door, Jack took a bullet to the leg and went down on one knee. Shy stopped to help him. He reached out the briefcase and handed it to Shy. "Go!" Jack said. "Take the money! I'll be alright," he said as he struggled to his feet.

Shy grabbed the money and looked around for Sean in the Escalade. There was no sign of it, so Shy began running toward the train station. She made it up the steps in time to see Mobley and Dylan come out. Jack fired at and hit one of them from across the street before ducking around the corner. Dylan went after Jack. Shy didn't wait to see if the other was coming after her; she made her way up the steps.

After paying her fair, Shy made it to the south side platform and hoped that the 4 train would come soon. Shy hid her gun under her jacket.

"Is this really the life you want to live?" she asked herself as she waited.

It was only ten minutes later when the train came down the tracks. Shy looked down the platform to see if she saw anybody. She got on the train and sat down thinking about the fact that she could take the train downtown and get off at 51st Street and Lexington Avenue. She could walk to the hotel from there. But the briefcase full of money said that getting off and taking a cab to the hotel was a better plan. She was going to get off at 161st and River Avenue at Yankee Stadium, but since there was no game that night, Shy stayed on until she got to 149th and Grand Concourse.

Shy got off the train and made it to the streets. She started walking toward the street to hail a cab, when out of the corner of her eye she saw Monk and Bailey come out of the train station. "Taxi!" she yelled and hoped it didn't get their attention.

A cab pulled up in front of her; she was about to get in when she heard the shot. Monk and Bailey were running toward her cab with guns drawn. Shy fired one shot and hopped in the cab. "Where to?" the taxi driver said calmly.

"Radisson on Lexington and 48th Street," Shy said. "And could you make it quick. I'm kinda in a hurry," she said; and the taxi disappeared into Grand Concourse traffic.

Chapter Twenty-eight

Rain was frantic and she didn't like it. She hadn't seen or heard from Nick in days; she didn't like that either. Her first thought was that he was with that bitch Wanda. She was so sure that he was at her house that she drove over there. Rain didn't see his car parked outside, but he could have parked blocks from there and walked back. She got out of the car and started for the house. If he was in there, she was going to put a stop to it right then and there.

Then Rain just stopped. *But suppose he ain't in there?* she thought. *Suppose I bust in there and the nigga ain't in there. I'll look like a fuckin' fool.*

Thinking it would be better if she caught him coming out the house, Rain went back to her car to wait.

When Wanda's driver arrived at seven A.M. sharp to take Wanda to an 8 o'clock meeting, Rain began thinking that maybe Nick wasn't there. But she sat there watching the house for another three hours before she was satisfied that Nick wasn't there.

Still convinced that this sudden disappearance had something to do with Wanda, Rain drove downtown to Wanda's office and spent the day watching the building, just in case he showed up there some time during the day. Later that evening after eight, she saw Wanda come out and get in her car, but still no sign of Nick. Her driver came around and got in the car. When they drove off, Rain was close behind. She sat outside Wanda's house until 10 o'clock before she finally started her car and drove away.

Where's this nigga at?

Maybe he's with one of his other women?

Rain looked at the time and hoped she could make it to the Fast Cash location that the light-eyed bitch, Tasheka, was manager of. A position Rain was sure Nick got for her. She got there just in time to see Tasheka come out and rush to her car.

Maybe she thinks she got a hot date with my man, Rain thought as she followed Tasheka to her house. An hour later, a car arrived at the house and a man got out and rang the bell. Tasheka had a hot date, but not with Nick, Rain was forced to admit as she drove off.

But Rain wasn't done, yet. She decided to drive by Cynt's to see if he was there with Mercedes. Rain got to Cynt's and went inside. As soon as Mercedes saw Rain come in, she excused herself from the client she was talking to and headed straight for Rain. She knew Rain couldn't stand her, and that made fuckin' with her all the better.

"Hey, Rain," Mercedes said and gave Rain what had become a customary kiss on the cheek.

Rain rolled her eyes. "What's up, Mercedes," she said, looking around the room for Nick.

Mercedes smiled and broke into a long story about two dancers who had gotten into a fight. It seems that one of the girls threw a drink in the other's face while she was dancing for a client. The fight got so bad that security had to break them up.

"Come to find out the girls is fuckin' each other, and the one that first threw the drink was just jealous. Now ain't that just the funniest shit you ever heard," Mercedes said and finally took a breath.

When Mercedes stopped talking, Rain looked at her with no expression on her face and said what she came to say, "You seen Nick tonight?"

"I haven't seen Nick for at least a couple of days. Which isn't like him at all," Mercedes said, and began moving away from Rain. "Gotta get back to work, honey. Make that money. You know what's up," she said and walked away laughing to herself.

Rain checked in with Cynt before she left and headed for J.R.'s. Even though she knew that Danielle was there working, she decided to make sure. As she expected, Danielle was at J.R.'s and Nick was nowhere to be found. Rain left J.R.'s and drove around to all their other spots, and nobody had seen Nick in days. She finally ended up at Jackie's. She sat down with Sonny Edwards and ordered a drink. "What's up, Sonny?"

"How's it going tonight, Rain?"

"Everything is cool." Rain looked around and didn't see him, and thought that there was no point in asking Sonny. "Where's Jackie and Travis tonight?" she asked instead.

"Neither one of them been here in a couple of days."

"What about Monika; you seen her?"

"Been a couple of weeks since Monika been around here."

Rain finished her drink. "Thanks, Sonny."

She left there and went back to J.R.'s and headed straight for her office. She passed by Rose, the club manager, and Rose said something to her, but Rain kept going. She went in her office and slammed the door. She flipped on the big screen; *Club Elite* with Misty Stone and Nyomi Banxxx was on. Rain tossed the remote and went to the bar to pour a shot of Patrón. She was about to pour her second drink when Rose knocked and came in. "What's bothering you?"

"What you mean?" Rain asked as she poured.

"You walked right by me and I was trying to tell you about what happened up here earlier, and you just kept walking like I hadn't said anything."

"Sorry, Rose. I got a lot on my mind, that's all."

"Well, pour me a drink and tell me about it," Rose said.

"I ain't seen or heard nothing from Nick, and you know that shit is fuckin' with me," Rain said as she poured a drink for Rose and refreshed her own.

"I ain't seen him, either. If he's in the city, it ain't like Nick not to come by here and check on things."

"That's what I'm saying. Then, come to find out, Monika, Travis and Jackie ain't been seen in days either."

"I know you told me that they all do different kinds of jobs together; maybe that's where he is."

"Yeah, I'll go along with that; but I'm usually part of that team too. Nick knows I hate to miss out on some gunplay. And even if that were the case, he would still tell me where they was going and shit. Or at least he woulda called by now and let me know what's up."

"I don't know what to tell you, girlfriend," Rose said.

"You ain't no fuckin' help." Rain laughed.

That left Rain to wonder if she had messed up when she left her cover position outside of the bank and came in. Then, Rain had broken radio silence and called for Jackie to drive the van through the front door. Even though doing so may have been the only thing that saved both the mission and their lives, she still disobeyed Monika's orders. Something she knew they took very seriously.

The next day, Rain made the drive out to Rockland County to talk to Bobby. Since Impressions was being rebuilt, Bobby went to South Carolina, got his kids, and had been working out of the house. After being so close to the explosion, Pam had a minor setback and now she was recovering.

"I'm just worried, Bobby, that's all," Rain said.

"I haven't heard anything and besides, with the whole group of them being gone, maybe they're doing something for Mike. You want me to call him?"

"No, that's all right. If they're doing something for Black, he'll tell me when he gets back." Rain said and got ready to leave. She felt like a schoolgirl with a crush and the shit was embarrassing, but what could she do.

Rain spent the rest of the day drifting from one bar to the next, trying to get drunk, but not really succeeding. She decided to go home, but found herself heading in the direction of the King family restaurant.

"I'm here to see Ronnie King," Rain said, and was taken back to the office and told that Mr. King was in a meeting, and was asked to wait. She made herself comfortable on the couch. It wasn't too long after that when detectives Kirkland and Bautista came in. Rain got up and practically curtsied.

"Good evening, Detective."

"Hello, Ms. Robinson. What are you doing here?" Kirk asked. He was genuinely surprised to see her sitting there, and not much surprised Kirk those days.

"Just visiting an old friend, Detective. Nothing major.".

Kirk was about to comment when somebody came out of the office. "Mr. King will see you now, detectives."

Kirk and Bautista walked away and went in the office. When Rain noticed that they had left the door cracked, she quietly made her way to listen.

"What can I do for you tonight, detectives?" Robert asked.

"I came to see if you or your son knows anything about a shootout on Burnside Avenue last night?" Kirk asked. "Three men were found dead and another was seen limping away from the scene."

Robert looked up at Ronnie. He shook his head. "Sorry, Detective. Like I said, I wouldn't know anything about those types of things. I run a legitimate business here."

"What about the deaths of Tree and Ramos Hurley, Antonie Edmonds, B Money, Donald Henderson, or Sly Stone? All of them were found dead too. I'm guessing that you haven't heard anything about any of those, either," Bautista said.

Robert laughed a little. "I never heard of any of those gentlemen."

Bautista leaned over the desk. "I didn't ask you if you heard of them; I asked you if you know anything about them being murdered?"

"No, Detective, I don't know anything about them being murdered. And I don't think I like the tone of your accusation."

"What you think?" Kirk began. "I'll tell you what I think. I think you know exactly what I'm talking about because you set it up. I think that eliminate and consolidate is exactly what an old *businessman* like you would come up with. So I'll tell you what I'm gonna do; I'm gonna use every resource I can muster to start digging into you, your son, and *every legitimate* business you got. I'm gonna sweat everybody that works for you, used to work for you, or even thought about working for you, until somebody, and there will be somebody, who knows something."

"How does that sound to you?" Bautista said as she started for the door. When Rain saw her coming, she moved quickly and reclaimed her spot on the couch.

When Kirk passed by, he told Bautista to go on and that he would catch up to her, and then he sat down next to Rain.

"I know you said that you're just visiting an old friend and I'm willing to except that. But you have a past reputation for being involved in their type of business. Now, my sources tell me, and I have received assurances from certain individuals that I have respect for, that you're not into that anymore."

"No, Detective. I run a nightclub now."

"Bullshit, Ms. Robinson. You're Mike Black's hammer," Kirk said, and Rain shut up. "So, I'm gonna give you a piece of advice; Stay away from these guys because I'm taking them down." Without another word, Kirk got up and left Rain sitting there. Rain sat a little bit longer when she noticed once again that the office door wasn't closed, so she eased back over there.

"Kirk knows something, or he wouldn't keep coming around," she heard Ronnie say.

"He doesn't know what he knows, and he hasn't got any evidence to back him up, or he'd have come with arrest warrants. And before he does, you need to get busy containing this, and find Monk and shut him down," Robert ordered.

"Yes, sir," Ronnie said and headed for the door. Rain rushed away from the door quickly, and had just made it to the couch when Ronnie came out. "Where you going? I mean, you're not leaving all ready, are you?"

"Yeah. I just came by to holla, but you took too long." Rain glanced at her watch. "I'm meeting with my managers at the club tonight and I need to go."

"You keep coming around here like this and I'm gonna start thinking you want me," Ronnie said and walked Rain out to her car.

"How many times I gotta say this; me and you can't be nothing but friends. I got a man. If and when that changes, I'll let you know," Rain said and shut her car door. She drove away thinking about what she had just heard and what it all meant.

Where is Nick when I need him?

Chapter Twenty-nine

Nick and his team parachuted into Sierra Leone, officially the Republic of Sierra Leone, a country in West Africa, at night, and made their way to the capital city, Freetown, which was founded in 1792 as a home for formerly enslaved black people. Sierra Leone is bordered by Guinea to the north and east, Liberia to the southeast, and the Atlantic Ocean to the west and southwest.

Freetown is located on a peninsula on the south bank of the estuary of the Sierra Leone River. The city lies at the foot of the Peninsula Mountains and faces one of the best natural harbors on the west coast of Africa. The peninsula is home to some of the finest beaches in Africa; Lumley Beach, Toke Beach, and Lakka Beach.

They checked into the Hotel Barmoi, which overlooked the ocean. The team spent the following day at Lakka Beach, which is 15 minutes from Lumley. Nick thought that everybody could use the day off after the long hike from the drop zone. He spent his day verifying the intel and reconnaissance. Later that evening they went over the mission again.

"It's a simple snatch and grab," Nick said when he called the team together. "For this mission, we maintain radio silence. Understood?"

"Understood," the team replied one by one.

"The objective, David Alexander, will come out of Embaixada da Franca here," he said and pointed to the map. "And then drive out onto Spur Road heading west. Xavier."

Xavier got up and moved toward the map. Nick handed him the pointer. "I'm in position on top of the building, here, with a clear shot of the snatch zone. I'm covering the mission with the .50 caliber Barrett M82," Xavier said.

"Travis."

He took the pointer from Xavier. "I pick the objective up there and follow. Keep him in sight, but don't get too close."

"Monika."

Travis bowed graciously and handed the pointer to Monika. "I come out from here and ease up alongside him," Monika said and handed Nick the pointer.

"I'm waiting here, in a spot directly below X. When I get the signal from X, I come out from there hard and block the objective. Monika stops alongside the objective and Travis closes the box behind him," Nick said and looked at Monika.

"I drop smoke bombs," she said.

"Travis."

"In the confusion, you, me, and Monika get out of our vehicles and eliminate his security and the driver. I shoot the one on the backseat with the objective. Monika, passenger in front is yours. Nick, you got the driver."

"Jackie."

"I pull up alongside."

"Monika." Jackie passed the torch.

"After I pop my guy," Monika began. "I open the back door, and pull out the objective and take him to Jackie. I get in with the objective and relieve him of the package."

"I should already be in the vehicle. My job is to provide you with cover," Nick said.

"Not to mention incentive for the objective to cooperate," Jackie added, and everybody laughed.

"By holding a gun to his head," Nick continued. "Travis."

"Once Jackie is away, I wait to pick up X, and then I assume a cover position."

"Jackie."

"I drive to the extraction point and we rendezvous there."

"Any questions?" Nick asked.

"More of a suggestion than a question," Monika said.

"What's that?"

"I know the Colonel selected the team for our skill set and by whose name appears next to what job. But I think that it may be better if me and X traded places."

"Reason?" Nick asked.

"I would hate to be the one to put the op in jeopardy because the objective was able to overpower me."

"She's got a point, Nick," Xavier said. "He does look like he is not going to go quietly, and they do want him alive."

"Right. And I think that I've proved that I'm just as good a sniper as X," Monika said with a definite sense of pride. While they were in Turkey the night before they parachuted into Sierra Leone, Monika and Xavier had a contest to see who the better sniper was. In the end, it turned out to be pretty even between the two shooters.

"X, you trade positions with Monica."

And it was set.

The following morning at 10:47, Dawud Iskandar, aka David Alexander, a former employee of the French company that manufactured the guidance system for the Milan 2: a surface-to-surface, guided missile, came out of Embaixada da Franca. Through his contacts, Dawud Iskandar obtained the guidance system and was currently leaving the country for a meeting with Al-Qadir, believed to be a moneyman for three violent extremist organizations operating on the continent. The meeting was set to take place in Nigeria the following day.

He came out of Embaixada da Franca with two bodyguards, the package handcuffed to his waist and chained to a briefcase, and got into a Toyota Hilux Surf SSR. Travis started the Daihatsu Terios CX the team was provided, to which Jackie said, "It's nice to not have to steal all the cars for a change."

He assumed his position and followed, and was soon joined by Xavier in a Toyota Landcruiser Prado SX, easing up alongside the objective. Monika was in position on top of a building and Nick was ready. He sat impatiently in the silver two-toned, diesel Mitsubishi Pajero. When he got the sign from Monika, Nick put on his gas mask, stepped on the gas, and broadsided the Hilux Surf.

Then, Xavier pulled up alongside them and was out the vehicle quickly. Travis moved in and prevented their escape. Xavier dropped two wire-pull smoke grenades, which produced a high volume of smoke for approximately ninety seconds.

The mission proceeded as planned. In the confusion that followed, Xavier moved quickly and shot the bodyguard in the front seat twice in the head while Nick eliminated the driver, as Travis did the same with the other bodyguard. Xavier opened the back door and pulled Iskandar out of the vehicle without any of the problems that Monika had anticipated occurring.

Jackie arrived on time in the escape vehicle: an M class Mercedes Benz. Nick got in and Xavier escorted Iskandar and put him in the backseat. Travis returned to his vehicle and waited to pick up Monika, who was making her way down.

A simple snatch and grab.

That's when it began to go wrong.

While Travis waited for Monika, he noticed that three cars with Chinese men inside, came through the dissipating smoke and were speeding to catch up with the Mercedes Jackie was driving.

Since they were in a foreign country, running an off the books op, Nick had insisted that they maintain radio silence; so Travis couldn't call and warn them. He sat waiting for Monika to come around the building. When he saw her, Travis got out and waved her on. Monika ran double-time to the vehicle and got in.

"What's up?"

"Three cars with Chinese men are in pursuit of Jackie," Travis said and took off behind them.

"You sure?"

"Absolutely."

"Shit! How far out are we?"

"Two ... maybe three minutes. What's the plan?"

"You catch them, and I'll stop them," Monika said, and wondered just how she'd do it.

Unaware they were being followed; Xavier took out a set of bolt cutters, which were not effective in breaking the chain on the handcuffs. Nick pressed the barrel of the gun a little harder against Iskandar's head. "I suggest you hold completely still," he recommended as Xavier used acid to cut through the chain.

Just then, one of the cars that were following opened fire and blew out the back window. All three men kept low. Xavier took a quick look. "Looks like at least two cars are on us. And they're coming up fast," he said and returned fire.

"Friends of yours?" Nick asked Iskandar as he pointed his gun.

"Undoubtedly, they want the same thing that you do," Iskandar told Nick.

"Get us outta here, Jackie."

"So what you think I'm doing up here, writing a love song," Jackie said as she increased her speed to get away from their pursuers.

About a half mile back, Travis and Monika sped to catch up with the rest of the team. "Do you see them?" Monika asked Travis as he made his way through traffic.

"Not yet."

"Open the sunroof!" Monika commanded. Once it was open, Monika stuck her head out, had a look around, and came back in. "They're about five car lengths ahead and they are taking incoming fire." When she came back up, Monika brought the .50 caliber Barrett M82 and set it up on the roof of the Daihatsu. "Get me closer," Monika yelled to Travis and took aim.

Travis stepped on the gas. When Monika was in range, she opened fire with the Barrett, knowing that her .50 caliber rounds would destroy the unarmored vehicles. The rounds cut through the car like butter, and it exploded. Travis drove through the smoke.

Nick heard the explosion and took a look. "Sounds like Monika's joined the party," he yelled as Xavier continued to fire at the oncoming vehicles.

"That would be good to know if these guys weren't still shooting at us," Xavier said and returned fire.

"Don't worry; Monika will get them off us," Nick promised.

"I know. I just hope she hurries," Jackie added as she weaved through traffic.

A slight smile washed over Monika's face as Travis closed in on the second of the three vehicles. She loved a good explosion, and gas tanks usually don't disappoint. Monika pulled the trigger, targeting the right rear of the vehicle. Her first volley hit the intended target, sliced through the gas tank, and blew out the rear tire. Monika kept firing as the car began to flip over in midair. The car came down front end first, but flipped over several more times before exploding upon final impact.

Monika stuck her head in. "Did you see that shit?" she yelled. "Did you fuckin' see that shit?" she yelled again; and Travis held up his hand without taking his eyes off the road to give her high-five. He had his eyes on the third car and didn't want to lose it in the smoke.

"One more to go!" Travis yelled.

The last car kept firing at the Mercedes. "Next time, you think they could get us an armored getaway car?" Jackie asked.

"You know if we were home I woulda had Chance hook it up," Nick said.

"If they're gonna make a habit of this, *Captain*, then we need to start bringing everything and everybody that we need to make these missions go right," Jackie said, and Nick knew that she was right. Having the support team in place always makes the mission go smoother.

Travis moved in on the third car and Monika took aim. "Get me closer!" Monika yelled, and Travis got her into perfect firing position. Once again, Monika targeted the gas tank and squeezed the trigger. The tank exploded and the car quickly engulfed in flames. Monika kept firing. Her second volley hit was to the engine and it exploded as Travis passed.

Jackie kept driving to the extraction point. When they got there, members of the United States Army took Dawud Iskandar into custody and flew him off in a military transport. The team boarded a helicopter and took off in the opposite direction.

ROY GLENN

Chapter Thirty

It was 12:15 P.M. when Delta flight 717 arrived in Nassau from Atlanta. Once the plane landed, Jada and her mother got up and gathered their things. They had been traveling since four-thirty that morning when Duke came for them in the limo. Jada insisted that they catch the flight at 6:15 A.M. so she could be back on the island as close to noon as she could.

"Why?" Vivian asked.

She wanted to hang out on their last night in New York, and then sleep in the next morning. "Then we could catch a later flight," she said.

"I have things to do on the island tomorrow afternoon," Jada explained. So they were up early and off to the airport; and after an almost ninety minute layover in Atlanta, they were in Nassau.

"This is your first time in the islands, isn't it, Mommy?"

"Yes. And it's beautiful," Vivian said as she looked out the window of the cab that took them to Sandy Port.

"I hope you like it down here and will think about staying," Jada said, and her mother turned and gave Jada an inquisitive look.

"You serious? You want me to stay down here in this paradise with you. Hell yeah, I wanna stay. What I'm going back to New York to do? Nothing but get in some trouble; and I know where that leads."

"Where?"

"Back to the penitentiary. And I got no plans on going back there." Vivian hugged her daughter and kissed her on the cheek. "Thank you, Jada. You just made this old hustler very happy."

Jada broke their embrace. "I just asked if you wanted to stay; no need for all this. You are so dramatic."

"No, Jada, you said more than that. You said, I love you, Mommy. Be a part of my world," Vivian said, and kissed Jada again as the taxi arrived at Sandy Port. Her eyes popped open at the sight of the pastel-colored villas inspired by the Georgian Colonial architecture that surrounded the marina.

"Is this yours, Jada?"

"It's not mine, but I do live here," Jada said with a sense of pride that she didn't think she'd feel.

"Baby, this is nice."

"Thank you," Jada said and opened the door to her three-bedroom suite. She stood back as Vivian wandered around the suite, taking in the large living and dining rooms, full kitchen, which had never been used, and the Jacuzzi.

"That is my room. So you can pick whichever of those two rooms you like," Jada said and began moving toward her room. "Make yourself at home. I've got to make a call and then I need to rush out. But I'll be back in a couple of hours and I'll show you the island and take you by Paraíso."

"What's that?"

"It's the business I told you about," Jada said and disappeared into the room. She picked up the phone and dialed.

"Hello."

"Good afternoon. Is Mike Black available?"

"Who should I say is calling?" M asked.

"Jada West."

"Hold on," M said and turned slowly toward Black, who was sitting at the table with the children waiting for Bernadette to serve lunch."

"Michael, phone for you." Black got up and came to the phone. M frowned. "Jada West."

"Business associate," Black said and took the phone. M wanted nothing more than to see him and Shy get back together. Another woman calling was not part of the rosy scenario that she had painted.

"Good afternoon, Ms. West."

"Good afternoon, Mr. Black. I wanted you to know that I was back on the island, and I was hoping that you were free for a late lunch?"

"What time?"

"Say, three o'clock?"

"That sounds good, Ms. West. I'll see you then."

"Splendid. Three o'clock then."

Black hung up the phone. He looked at M; she looked at him. She wanted to ask who Ms. West was, but she thought better of it. Black went back to eat lunch with his children. After lunch, he let them play for a while before he told them it was nap time.

When Jada arrived at their room at the Hilton for lunch, to her surprise, Black was there waiting for her. "Well, this is a surprise," she said as she walked slowly into the room. "You must have missed me."

Black stood up and walked toward her. "I wasn't doing too much and ..." Black began and then he thought about it. "Yeah, I missed you." He stopped in front of her. "More than I really want to admit. More than I want to admit to you."

"You just missed Ms. Kitty," Jada said and smiled at him.

"No, it's more than that, Ms. West. I missed you ... all of you. I missed our time together."

Jada threw her arms around him and kissed him. "Oh, Mr. Black, I missed you so much. There were days when I felt like I would die because I couldn't talk to you every day; when I couldn't feel you inside me."

"You could have called," he said, and then Black thought about whom he was talking to. "Did you enjoy your time with your mother?"

"Yes, I did. In fact, she's here on the island. If you come to Paraíso tonight, I'll introduce you. But she says she knows you from the old days."

"Really? I don't think I remember meeting Lucas West's wife."

"Well, like I said, she says she knows you."

"I guess I'll see tonight." Black sat down on the bed. "How was it to see her after ten years?"

"I was a little uncomfortable at first, and she was acting like I had seen her the week before or something. That went on for a couple of days, and then we finally got around to talking about it; and that's all we've talked about since. It made me realize that after she said that she didn't want to have any contact with me, that that was when I began to separate myself from my feelings."

"I thought that was something that you did when you started working with Sasha?"

"I thought so, too, but now that I have to see her and deal with it, I realize that is where it began. Working with Sasha, and her telling me that it was easier to do the work if you detach yourself from your feelings, just gave me a reason for doing what I was already doing. That's how I was able to walk around that dive naked and dance in a room full of horny men. Something I thought I'd never do. But it came so easy to me; and that was because I'd already cut off that part of myself, when she said she didn't want to hear from me anymore. I never thought I'd see Vivian West again."

"Looks like now the two of you have a second chance."

"That's just it, Mr. Black; I don't want to feel the way this whole thing has me feeling. I don't want to leave myself open like that. Let your guard down for a minute, and people will hurt and disappoint me the first chance they get, is what Sasha used to say."

"I don't know what to tell you about that, Ms. West."

"And you of all people shouldn't try."

"Why is that?"

"Because you top the list of people that could hurt me, and hurt me badly, if I opened myself up and allowed myself to feel all of the things I could feel for you."

"That I understand."

"I want you so badly, even though I know fully what your situation is. You are actively trying to get back with your wife. And it's just a matter of time before she comes to her senses and you and I have to have that talk. And I am not looking forward to that."

"What do you want me to say?"

"Honestly, Mr. Black, there is nothing for you to say. Anything you said right now, with you making admissions to me that you actually missed me and not just my sex, would only drive those feelings to the surface."

"What should we do?"

"You should make love to me right now. Don't say another word, just undress me and I'll undress you, and then make love to me."

Black smiled. "I can do that."

After they made love, as they always did, Black and Jada went their separate ways; knowing that they'd see each other again later that evening. Jada returned to Sandy Port where Vivian was waiting.

"Was it good?" Vivian asked when Jada came through the door.

"I beg your pardon."

"I asked you if it was good."

"I'm sure I don't know what you're talking about."

"Who you think you're fooling, child. I am not only a woman, I'm your mother. Shit. The way you ran outta here, only one thing can do that to a woman ... some good dick."

"Since you seem to already know, I don't have to say anything."

Vivian lit a cigarette. "Damn right. That was something I used to know about."

"I'm sure," Jada said and sat across from her.

"What's that supposed to mean?" Vivian asked.

"I didn't mean anything by it. Honestly, Mother, don't read too much into things."

"All right now. Don't be walking around here thinking just 'cause you made it that you can talk shit about what I had to do. Damn right, I would do whatever it took to make money."

"Yes, Mother, I know," Jada said and imitated her mother's voice. "Honey, when you got a man's back, I mean truly got his back, a woman gotta step up. Sometimes a woman gotta use what she got to get what she gotta get to take care of her family."

"Sometimes it was more than just sometimes," Vivian said and took a long drag.

"What are you saying?"

"That there were times, especially early on, that your daddy would come home with less money than he left with. Then when he got better shooting pool, nobody wanted to play him. Who you think kept a roof over our heads and food on the table? It was me doing what I had to do; using what I had to get what we needed to survive."

"Is that why when he had a woman on the hook that he was getting money from, you wouldn't say anything?"

"Now you're starting to understand that for me and your daddy, God bless him, it was always about the money. 'Cause no matter who or where we were getting money from, it was all for us."

"We were always a family."

"That's why I didn't want you to come see me or even hear from me."

"Why?"

"Because it was the same, if not worse, on the inside. The big butch inmates, the guards, both male and female, the counselors, were supposed to have been there to help you. Shit! They all want the same thing. To them, I was just somebody else to prey on. Somebody else they could use and abuse to get what they wanted. I didn't want you to know anything about any of that. It was too painful to go through; but I did what I had to do to get through it. I'm not proud of the things I did, but it's over and behind me and I'm happy to be here with you. But I'll be honest, the only thing that kept me going was thinking about you."

"Then why did you cut me off the way you did?"

"I didn't want you to know what I had to do to survive in there." Vivian laughed. "I can't tell you how many times I read your letters like I was getting them for the first time. It's what got me through that hell."

"Wow. That's all I can say right now. I'm sorry you had to go through that. Now I feel selfish."

"Why?"

"Mommy, look around. Sure, I've done some things ... shook my ass, sold my body, but I've had a relatively good life. Now I feel bad that you had to go through that."

There's that word again, Jada thought.

ROY GLENN

Feel.
And the last thing I want to do is feel.

179

Chapter Thirty-one

"The other night while we were out, BB, you asked me if I had an opinion. Well, here it is. The program you're running is sloppy and it ends today."

It seemed like every brain cell in CeeCee's head was on fire and sparking all at the same time. She had been a baller's woman for years. Now every conversation she had ever heard, everything that she'd been told in passing; everything that she saw during all those years was coming to her. As she sat there talking to BB, Dex and Lightman, it was like she was outside herself looking down and marveling at what she was saying.

Early that same morning, CeeCee had breakfast with Detective Mulligan from Lieutenant Sanchez's narcotics squad and handed $10,000 to him. Before she got involved with Cash Money, she used to deal with a guy that they called Kick. She moved on to Cash when 'The Kicker,' as some were known to call him, was murdered in the streets. She remembered him saying, "If you want to run a tight program you gotta treat people right, and spread the money around. And that includes the cops. Everything goes better when everybody is happy, 'cause they making paper."

CeeCee remembered that the cop that Kick used to deal with always liked her and would flirt with her. Until Kick told him that if he so much as looked at CeeCee again, he would put two in his chest.

"Then I'll sit there and wait for the cops to come take me away for murdering one of their own," she remembered Kick telling Mulligan.

He was surprised when CeeCee walked into the place where Mulligan always had breakfast and used to meet Kick. Before the breakfast meeting was over, Mulligan had agreed to provide CeeCee with protection from the cops and information about them.

"Starting today, all the spots we run, all the people that work for us, are going to do things the same way," CeeCee continued. "Dex."

"Yeah."

CeeCee smiled sweetly at him. "I was watching the way you ran your show and I was impressed. That is going to be how every spot gets run. Anybody who can't get with that, we don't need them. Call them rules, call them policies and procedures ... hell ... call them the commandments if you want to, it doesn't matter. Just as long as everybody knows them and follows them to the letter."

CeeCee knew that having Dex onboard with what she was saying would be crucial to its success. Every now and then, CeeCee would glance over at Dex to gauge his reaction to what she was saying. To this point, she could tell that Dex was thinking; *Who does this bitch think she's talking to.* "And honestly, Dex, your talents are wasted sitting on the hood of some car all night."

"What you have in mind?"

"I think that you are the perfect man to make sure that everyone that works for us is on the same page. In other words, you come up with the rules based on the way you were running your show, and make sure everybody else does too."

Dex gave CeeCee a little smile and nodded his head. "I can do that."

"Lightman."

"Yes, ma'am."

"Don't call me that. I ain't your mother. Anyway, from now on, I want you to be in charge of security for our entire operation. That means you need to get started recruiting muscle. These guys will have no contact with product. If they got a drug charge on their records, we can't use them. I took steps this morning to insure that the police will not be an issue."

"How you manage that?" BB wanted to know.

"I got a cop on the payroll. Lightman, part of your responsibility is to deal with him. Narc named Mulligan."

"Who is that?" BB asked.

"Just another greedy cop; so you make sure that you keep plenty of money in his hands. Can you handle that for us?" CeeCee asked.

"I can do that." Lightman promised.

"What the fuck am I going to do?" BB demanded to know.

"I want you to do what you're best at." CeeCee began.

"What is that?" Dex asked and laughed a little.

"Nothing," Lightman said, and everybody laughed but BB.

"BB, your job is recruitment and expansion," CeeCee said when she stopped laughing. "I mean, that is what you're always talking about; expansion, right?"

"Right, right."

"You find and bring us the guys out there that are making money, but aren't connected to anybody. That's how we expand. Slowly, so we can manage the growth; not just jump out there like the rest of these niggas that are ending up dead."

"I know that's right," Dex said.

"I ain't trying to get dead or go to jail over this thing we're doing. I'm here to make money," CeeCee said. "That's all I got. Anybody got a problem with or a question about anything I just said?" she asked and waited for somebody to say, "Who put you in charge?"

Nobody said a word.

"Good. Since we are all in agreement, let's go make this money." Then she remembered something. "Oh yeah, there is somebody that I want to bring in. He goes by the name Blunt," CeeCee informed her new team.

"I heard of him, but I don't know him," BB said. "What he gonna do?"

"Watch my back," CeeCee said and got up.

Now all she had to do was tell Blunt what she was doing. Lay out her program and convince Blunt to go along with her. The first phase of that happening would begin later that evening when Blunt picked her up for dinner.

At six that night, Blunt called and said that he was having some problems and wanted to cancel, but CeeCee had an agenda, so she insisted that whenever he was done dealing with his problems, that he call her. "We can grab something to eat and do something," she told him.

"That's okay, Cami. It might be late, and I know you got a business to run in the morning."

"You see, that's the advantage of being the boss. You get to come in when you want to, leave when you want to, and do whatever you want when you get there."

"So, you got it like that, huh?"

"If you didn't know that by now, somebody should have told you," CeeCee said confidently. "So it doesn't matter what time it is, you come get me."

It was after ten that night when Blunt called and said that he was on his way. So she wouldn't have to hear anymore of her mother's mouth, she was outside sitting on the stoop when he got there. "Hey, handsome," CeeCee said when she got in his car.

"Sorry I took so long, Cami."

"It's okay. I'm just glad you made it. It's been so long since I've seen you."

"I been mad busy, Cami. Sometimes I just don't have time to do all the things I want to. The more pleasurable things."

"Did you work out your problems?" CeeCee asked.

"Let's just say I worked around them for the time being," Blunt said. "So, you still wanna grab something to eat?"

"Honestly, dude, I'd be cool with a couple of slices from the pizza joint up on two thirty-third," CeeCee said.

"That's it?"

"Okay, you can buy me a grape soda to go with it, but only if you're good."

A short time later, they were being served their slices. CeeCee bit into hers. "I swear ... this is the best pizza in the world."

"It's all right," Blunt said. "But, best in the world, Cami, I don't know about that."

"Trust me, by the time you finish them slices, you'll be standing here testifying," CeeCee said and held up her right hand.

"Yeah, we'll see."

"So, tell me about these problems of yours that kept me waiting for four hours."

"You don't wanna hear about all that madness."

"Yes, I do, really. You never know, I might be the answer to all of your problems."

"Wouldn't that be something," Blunt said, making light of her statement. But CeeCee was serious, so she pushed a little harder.

She ran her hand gently across his cheek. "Look at it this way, handsome; you have nothing to lose by telling me." CeeCee wanted to add, "And everything to gain", but she held back just in case he had some shit going on that she wanted no parts of. And if that was the case, she could say, "That's too bad", and quickly change the subject.

"You serious, you really wanna hear this?"

"Yes, I really do."

"Okay. What it comes down to is I'm having a run of bad luck," Blunt began. "At least I hope it's just bad luck. But the last three days have been three fucked-up days."

"What happened?"

"First off, this nigga Tree I was buying from fucked around and got dead on me. Now my supply is drying up. What made it worse is that the cop busted two of my boys in a bullshit traffic stop, and they was carrying weight, so I lost people and product. This chick named Knives said she could step in with some product, but I hear that her and her partner, another chick called Babygirl are grimy."

"I know them bitches, they just setting you up so they can rob you," CeeCee said.

"That's what the word I get is."

"You might wanna shoot them two snakes on sight. You'd be doing a public service." CeeCee was about to go into the pitch she'd been practicing, but Blunt wasn't done.

"On top of all that, I got some young niggas trying to push me off my corners. And you know how these young niggas are; they gonna make me catch a case fuckin' around with them."

CeeCee smiled as she thought about how perfect this was. She decided to drop the prepared speech and go straight to her offer. "Suppose I were in a position to offer you solutions to some, if not all, of your problems?" CeeCee asked.

"Like what?"

"Let's just say for the sake of this conversation that I could offer you a quality product at a competitive price that you can make money with, protection from the police and security for your people. If I could offer you that, would you be interested?"

"That depends, Cami."

"On what?"

"Whether I would still have control?"

"Of course you would. Other than some minor changes to make things run smoother, you would operate any way you saw fit. Would that be worth it to you to get on board?"

"If you were, for conversation sake, able to offer that, I might be interested."

"Well. That is exactly what I'm offering you."

"You're kidding me, right?"

"Not at all. Everything I just offered you is in place or soon will be."

"Okay, I'm interested, but let me try to work this out for myself. I gotta see a man named Nico Dees tomorrow night. If that works out, it will go a long way toward me working things out for myself. If not, and you can really do all you say, yeah, consider me on board."

"I'll see you tomorrow then," CeeCee said.

Chapter Thirty-two

Shy was alone in her room pacing back and forth. It had been two days since the shootout and she still hadn't heard anything from Jack. She had given up on calling him the day before and had been out all day looking for him, and nobody else had seen or heard from him, either.

Is he dead? Did the cops catch him? She didn't know.

Although she was very worried about Jack, there was a part of her that thought that maybe this was the best thing that could have happened to her. It forced her to answer the tough questions that she'd been asking herself from the start, but had been avoiding the answer to.

Is this really what you want your life to be, drug deals and shootouts? Shy thought back to the last time she went to do business. *That ended the same way this did; me shooting my way outta there. Only difference was, that time I ended up getting shot and damn near dying in Bobby's back seat.*

Shy couldn't tell how many times since that night she'd asked herself; *What would have happened if Michael hadn't sent Bobby to follow me? Would E's fake cops have killed me? Would the real cops have caught me? Or would I just have died in the street from loss of blood?*

It wasn't that long ago that Shy was sure that she was going to die alone on the island. Now it seemed like she was in a rush to die in the streets.

You know that's all that's out there, right? Dead or in jail for twenty years.

She thought about Michelle. *I have a second chance to raise my daughter; watch her grow up.* And if that were the case, what was she doing in New York when Michelle was in the Bahamas with her father. Then she thought about Black. Despite the games she was playing with him, Shy knew that she loved him and wanted to spend the rest of her life loving him.

And if that were really true, what am I doing up here when Michael is in the Bahamas with our daughter?

Shy knew that it was time to put a stop to this foolishness before this life she had chosen to lead, got her killed or locked up. It was time to go home. But Shy felt like she couldn't leave until she knew what had happened to Jack. She grabbed her gun and headed out the door.

That same night, somebody else was searching their soul for answers to the future, and had come to the same conclusion. Leon decided that he'd had enough. With dealers coming up dead left and right, the threat of Monk trying to move on him was becoming a real possibility. That, or Sanchez getting a warrant for his arrest. He talked it over with Diamond and Pearl and they agreed.

"We've made enough money," Pearl said. "It's time to call it a day."

"Pearl's right. Only place we can go from here is to jail or the morgue," Diamond added.

"We out then," Leon said.

"Where we going?" Pearl asked.

"Eventually, we'll end up in Aruba; but we got a stop to make before we go there."

"Where to?" Diamond asked.

"Nassau," Leon said, and Pearl ran her tongue over her lips at the thought of seeing Mike Black again.

The three arrived in Nassau and were met at the airport by Jamaica's men. They were taken to the Yellow Rose and were escorted directly to the pool where Black was in the water playing with the kids.

"This is something I never thought I'd see. Mike Black as daddy," Leon said as he walked to the edge of the pool to greet Black.

"Honestly, Leon, I never thought I'd see me playing this part, either, but here I am. And you know what?"

"What's that?"

"Ain't nothing better than being with your kids," Black told him. He turned to Diamond and Pearl. "Hello, ladies."

"Hey, Black," Diamond said.

"How are you, Mike?" Pearl asked.

"Like I said, it doesn't get any better than this."

"How's the water?" Pearl asked.

"The pool is heated, so the water is fine. You ladies are welcome to change into your swimwear and join us."

"Where can we change?" Diamond asked.

"Go through that glass door. Bernadette should be in the kitchen. If not, just holla for her. She'll show you to your rooms," Black said as Leon dragged a chair closer to the pool.

While they were gone to change, Leon told Black that he was getting out of the drug business.

"Retire ... you? Now that's something I thought I'd never see. I thought that you was in for life."

"Me either; but things in New York are getting too wild. Lieutenant Sanchez has become my best friend ever since I been back in the city."

Black laughed. "What's up with that?"

"I told you about when him and Kirk came to Nina's apartment and found me there."

"Sanchez is relentless."

"I ain't that stupid that I can't see that it's only a matter of time before he shows up at my door with an arrest

189

warrant. My daddy, my uncles, my cousin Lo, all of them doing time; I just ain't trying to join them."

"Smart man. So what you gonna do?"

"After we leave here, we're going to Aruba."

"Sounds good. But the question still stands; what you gonna do, Leon? I know if you don't have something to do, what we do will draw you back in."

"A friend of mine from Jacksonville bought some land and built a resort, and he let me buy in. It's called the Yahnica Beach Resort & Spa."

"No shit."

"No shit. The ultimate Caribbean vacation experience begins at this intimate, two-story boutique resort located on the shores of Eagle Beach. It is an ideal place for romantic and rejuvenating getaways," Leon said, quoting what he'd read repeatedly on the brochure.

"You got the shit down."

"Shhh. Now let me finish my presentation." Leon laughed.

Black held up his hand in surrender.

"You relax beside the Caribbean Sea on a breathtaking stretch of beach. The hotel has seventy-one deluxe rooms with bathrooms that have waterfall showers."

"I need to check that out."

"Yeah, me too. The beach resort got three restaurants. It's got all that shit like free Wi-Fi and Internet terminals in each room; two pools, fitness room, yoga classes and a spa on the beach," Leon said as Diamond and Pearl returned to the pool wearing their bikini's.

"That sounds great, Leon. I hope that it works out for you."

"I been seeing how this island life agrees with you. I just thought maybe it's for me too."

"Well, I'm glad you came to tell me about it," Black began, but Leon cut him off.

"That ain't the only thing I came here to tell you about," Leon said.

"What else?"

"I need to talk to you about his mama," Leon said and pointed at Easy, "and her mama." He pointed at Michelle.

"What about them?"

"I don't think they need to hear this," Leon said.

Black turned quickly to Michelle. "Michelle, take your brother and go in the house."

"Why, Daddy?"

"Because I need to talk to Uncle Leon," Black said with a stern look on his face. "Now go on and do what I told you to do."

Pearl stood up. "That's okay, Mike; you go on and talk to Leon. Auntie Pearl will get in the water with them," she said and got in the pool and made her way to the children. Black got out.

Leon explained to Black what Shy and CeeCee were doing. Black went in the house and started to tell M to pack up the kid's stuff, but quickly changed his mind. "I'm going to New York for a couple of days. Do you mind staying here with the children?"

"Is something wrong, Michael?" M asked.

"Why do you ask?"

"You know I hate it when you answer my question with a question. Ever since you were young, I always thought you were trying to keep something from me."

"Will you take care of them, Ma?"

"Of course I will."

191

"Thanks, Ma," Black said and kissed his mother on the cheek. Then he called the airport and arranged a charter. Then he called Bobby.

Chapter Thirty-three

If there was one thing that was certain about Kirk, he was a man of his word. Not only were Kirk and Bautista all over the King's people with questions, he had uniform officers arresting them for petty charges ranging from loitering to open containers. They'd get arrested; the detectives would question them and then release them. So far, nobody knew anything that Kirk hadn't figured out for himself. But he was confident that it was just a matter of time before somebody handed him something that he could use.

For Robert King, it had been a hard couple of days. Kirk was also bringing in the King's legitimate staff for questioning as well. He looked up at Ronnie when he came in the office.

"I really fucked this one up."

"What do you mean, Pop? It was a solid plan and well executed. I know when things quiet down it will all pay off in the end."

"I believe that too. Only thing is that instead of worrying about Mike Black, I should have been more concerned about Kirk."

"Don't worry. Eventually he'll lose interest or move on to another case, and things will quiet down."

"That's just it. Kirk won't lose interest; and even if he picks up another case, he'll still find time to harass us," Robert told Ronnie.

"What are we gonna do?" Ronnie asked.

"All we can do is ride it out."

It was getting late in the evening and Detective Bautista was thinking about calling it a night. More to the point, she was thinking about inviting Kirk to have a drink with her, but he had other plans. "Where you headed?" Bautista asked when she noticed that they weren't on their way to the precinct.

"There's somebody I wanna talk to before we head in for the night," Kirk said, as they passed by four men standing on the corner.

"Who is that?"

"Guy named Jon Anderson."

"And who is that?"

"He's one of my snitches. One of my more reliable ones at that," Kirk said as he drove.

"If he so reliable, why are we just getting around to talking to him?"

"Sensible question."

"Do you have a sensible answer?"

"I do. He was at Rikers on a drug charge; I didn't know that he was back on the street," Kirk said as he made a U-turn.

When they saw the car coming toward them, the men scattered. Kirk stopped the car short and he and Bautista jumped out and followed Anderson. It didn't take Kirk long to catch up with him. He grabbed him by the collar and tossed him to the ground.

"Where you going in such a hurry, Anderson?" Kirk asked as he pulled him up. He pushed him against the wall and searched him. He pulled out a dime piece of heroin.

Kirk handed the bag to Bautista. "What do we have here?" she asked, dangling the bag in front of his face.

"Come on, Kirk, give me a break!" Anderson yelled.

"What can you tell me about the drug dealer killings?"

"What do you want to know?"

"Let's start with who's behind it?"

"I don't know!"

ROY GLENN

Kirk took the bag from Bautista, dropped it on the ground, and stepped on it. "Cuff him and read him his rights, Bautista," Kirk ordered.

Bautista took out her cuffs.

"I do know that whoever it was brought in out of town muscle to put in the work. Some heavy hitter from Cleveland; goes by Monk. I swear, Kirk, that's all I know."

"Not good enough. I wanna know where I can find this guy," Kirk said, and Bautista put the cuffs on.

"You have the right to remain silent," Bautista began.

"Wait a minute, wait!"

"Where do I find these guys?" Kirk yelled in his face.

"I don't know where Monk is, but two of his cowboys were at the Ramada on Baychester.

Kirk let go of Anderson and Bautista took off the cuffs. Kirk stuck a twenty in Anderson's shirt pocket and then walked away. Anderson looked at the twenty and understood why he played the game with Kirk.

When Kirk got back to the precinct, he sat down at his desk and pulled his rolodex closer. He flipped through it until he found the card he was looking for. "Homicide.

"Detective Wilenza, please."

"Speaking."

"Wilenza, this is Detective Kirkland from New York. We served on that task force together."

"Sure, I remember you. What can I do for you?" Wilenza asked.

"I'm trying to get some info about one of your model citizens."

"You got a name?"

"Goes by Monk."

"And what a model citizen he is. Thelonious Johnson aka Monk," Wilenza told Kirk.

"Real name is Thelonious Johnson," Kirk said to Bautista, and she started to pull him up on her computer. "What can you tell me about him?" he asked.

"That he's a murdering psychopath. That, and if you got him there, keep him."

"For life ..." Kirk paused. "In prison. Thanks."

"Anytime, Kirk."

"What you get?" Kirk asked.

"Thelonious Johnson aka Monk; plenty of arrests, only two convictions; one for aggravated assault, served five of ten; and a murder charge. Served twelve and got out on parole. I got a mug shot," Bautista said and hit print.

"We need known associates."

"Got them," she said; and the detectives were out the door and on their way to the Ramada on Baychester. They showed the manager the pictures of Monk and his associates.

"These two," the manager said.

"What room?" Bautista asked.

"Two seventeen."

Upon arrival on the second floor, the detectives knocked on the doors of the rooms around 217 and got the guests in the surrounding rooms out. Once the other guests were out, Kirk and Bautista positioned themselves on either side of the door. He banged on the door.

"Police!" Kirk yelled.

The response he got was shooting through the door. Kirk waited for a lull in the gunfire, and then he kicked in the door. Bautista went in low and fired at Dylan who was hiding behind the bed, reloading. He aimed and Bautista fired twice. She hit him with both shots; the second of which was fatal. Mobley was unarmed. He put up his hands and surrendered to Kirk.

ROY GLENN

When backup arrived, Kirk walked Mobley out in handcuffs and took him to the precinct for questioning. Once Kirk explained that he was looking at six life sentences and, "Maybe even the death penalty," he also added. He quickly gave up that he was working with Monk and where to find him, and that Monk was working for some guy named King.

A TALE OF THREE WOMAN

Chapter Thirty-four

That afternoon, Bobby was waiting outside when Black's charter taxied to the building. Before he left the island, he called Jada and told her that he wouldn't be by Paraíso that night. And he told her that he had some business in New York and would call her when he got back. He thought it was best, after the conversation they had that afternoon, not to mention that he was going to New York to find Shy.

Jada was right about him, he wanted nothing more than for Cassandra to, as Jada had said, "Come to her senses," and then he and Jada would have to have that talk. He had really begun to have feelings for Jada West. He wasn't in love with her though; at least he didn't think he was. But from the first time he saw her on stage dancing at Ecstasy, there was always something about Jada West that moved him in ways that no woman ever had, and that included Shy.

He wondered at times whether even if Shy did come back to him, if he would be able to stay away from Jada. Each time he thought about it, the question went unanswered. And then she went and complicated things.

You top the list of people that could hurt me and hurt me badly, if I opened myself up and allowed myself to feel all of the things I could feel for you.

It was easier to think that it was just sex to her and that she felt nothing, than to believe that the reason Jada did things the way she did was to protect herself from being hurt by those feelings.

But this wasn't the time to worry about what to do about Jada West. He had to worry about what the other two women in his life were up to. Black got off the plane and Bobby walked up to him. He looked around. "Where are the

198

kids?" Bobby asked, expecting that Black was returning the children to their mothers.

"They're in Nassau with M," Black said.

"Oh, shit," Bobby took out his gun and put one in the chamber, "what's wrong?"

"You heard anything about Cassandra and CeeCee selling drugs?"

"Together?"

"Hell no. At least I don't think they're working together." Black paused and thought about it. "No. If that were the case, Leon would have mentioned it."

"Hold up now, Mike. Why don't you start at the beginning," Bobby said as they walked to his car.

"Leon came to see me today." Black began and recounted what Leon had told him.

"No, Mike, sorry. I haven't heard anything like that."

"Cassandra I'm not surprised about. That's all she knows, but Cee? I just can't wrap my mind around that one."

"Was Leon sure?"

"He was," Black said as they got in Bobby's car.

"Where to?"

"Cassandra is staying at the Radisson on Lexington and Forty-eighth."

"That's as good a place as any to start. But I'm still tripping on CeeCee being a drug dealer. I'm like you; I just can't see it."

The first place they went was to the Radisson. Black knocked on Shy's door, but he had a feeling that he was wasting his time. As he expected, there was no answer.

"What now?" Bobby asked.

"Let me use your phone, Bobby."

"No can do. I banned cell phone use for everybody."

"Good idea, but why?"

"I read somewhere that cell companies are just giving shit to the cops. Shit like location information, text messages, and something they called cell-tower dumps. That's where any calls made through a tower for a certain period of time, they don't need a warrant for. When I heard that shit I banned them."

"Smart move."

"Face-to-face conversations only."

"Okay, take me to find Jap. I need him in the street looking for them."

"You got it," Bobby said and drove toward Jap's apartment. When they got there, Black just told Jap to find them, but he didn't say why. "And see if you can run down a guy named Jack."

"The one that used to roll with her?"

"The same," Black said before leaving out with Bobby. "Meet me at Doc's in two hours."

"I'll be there," Jap said, and everybody left the apartment.

Now that Jap was up and running, Bobby asked once again, "Where to?"

"Take me to see Angelo."

"Why him?" Bobby never did like Angelo and for the life of him, he couldn't understand why Black did.

"That's who Cassandra would go to first for product."

"If she didn't turn to him, where would she go?"

"Hector maybe, or one of his people. After that, I have no idea," Black said.

"I thought her boy Jack was still in jail over their shit?"

"Just got out."

"I follow you now. If she's back in the game, he's in it with her."

"Glad I didn't have to break that down for you."

"But it's like you said, I get it with Shy. That shit is in her blood. You know it's hard to break from that."

"Yeah, I know. Look at us. We've made a bunch of money all these years. We don't have to do this shit."

"Right. But here we are, about to get in the street; and you know what usually happens when we hit the street."

"Somebody gets dead. So nobody understands that better than me. What I'm trying to make her see is that we got a daughter now. I got a son that I'm gonna get if Cee is really involved in the game on any level."

"What you gonna do?"

"I'm just gonna keep him down there with me. Easy is a Bahamian citizen; so let her get a lawyer and come fight me down there for him. But for some reason, I don't think she will," Black said. "But what I gotta make Cassandra understand is that both of us can't be in the streets, preferably neither one of us needs to be in these streets, taking chances that may cause Michelle to lose one or maybe even both of us. Truth is, now that she's back, I can't stand to lose her again, Bobby. And I will do whatever I have to do to keep that from happening."

"I'm with you. Since we talking truth here, I might as well be retired. This is the first time I been to the city since you left. I make Nick and Wanda come out there to talk to me. They tell me what's up; I ask them what they think we should do. If it sounds reasonable, I tell them to go ahead. If not, I tell them what to do and send them back to the city. If it's something major, I come down there and kick it around with you."

"What, did you think there was some rocket science or Jedi magic to this?" Black asked as they arrived at the private social club that Angelo operated from. Black and Bobby both surrendered their weapons, a house rule, and were escorted to Angelo's office.

"Mikey, Bobby, how's everybody doing tonight?"

"I'm good, Angee. What about you?" Black asked.

"About the same as always." Angelo smiled. "You know it took you awhile; longer than I expected actually. But I knew sooner or later you'd be coming."

"Then you know what I want."

"Let's walk outside, Mikey? There may be unwelcome ears in here. You never know, right? Better safe than back in fuckin' jail," Angelo said quietly.

Black and Angelo walked down the street with Bobby and two of Angelo's men close behind.

"Shy came to me and asked me to put her on to somebody she could do business with."

"Did you?"

"Of course I did. That's business, Mikey."

"I got no issue with that, Angee. You're a business man. Somebody comes to you to do business, you do business."

"I knew you would understand. I put her in touch with Nicolò De Luca."

"Nico Dees. Where can I find him?"

"In the cemetery. Somebody popped Nico a couple of weeks ago. I'm guessing she turned to somebody else after that, because I ain't hear from her."

"When were you planning on telling me all this?"

"When you asked," Angelo said, and Black looked confused. "She said, and I quote, Michael does not know what I'm doing, and I would prefer that you didn't mention it to him. I told her that if you asked me a question, I'm gonna answer you honestly. And when you ask me why didn't I tell you, I'm gonna tell you that Shy asked me not to. I told her that I wouldn't lie to you. And she was good with that."

Black shook Angelo's hand. "You're an honorable man, Angee. You wouldn't betray her confidence, and honored our friendship at the same time."

"That's what honorable guys do, Mikey," Angelo said.

Their next stop was to CeeCee's house. He didn't expect to find her there either, but you never know, right. Black rang the bell and soon Mrs. Collins yelled, "Who is it?"

"It's Mike Black, Mrs. Collins," he said, and she opened the door.

"How are you, Michael? Come in," she said looking around for Easy.

"This is Bobby Ray, Mrs. Collins."

"It's good to meet you, ma'am."

"Good to meet you too, Mr. Ray." She turned to Black. "I wasn't expecting you for another few days. Is everything all right?"

"Everything is fine. I'm just looking for Cee. Do you know where I can find her?"

"I have no idea where she is."

"Well when you see her, please tell her I'm here in New York and I'm looking for her," Black said and started to leave.

Mrs. Collins stopped him. "Michael, I know what goes on between the two of you is none of my business and I've tried to stay out of her way since she's been back, but I don't think she realizes, and we've had this conversation before, that she has a son to raise now. I know that you take that responsibility very seriously. So I know that whatever it is that's going on was enough to get you to leave that boy and come up here, must be important."

"I think it is."

"Come on back in and sit down, Michael. I think you and I need to talk."

Black and Bobby looked at each other and then followed Mrs. Collins into the living room.

"I am glad you're here," Mrs. Collins said.

"Is something wrong?" Black asked.

"I don't know if wrong is the right word, but I know that whatever Cameisha is doing, there is something that just doesn't feel right about it to me. I mean, she done fell back in with some fool she used to run around with before he went to jail."

"Who is that, Mrs. Collins?"

"I don't know his name, but she calls him Blunt. Now come on, with a name like that, what you think he's doing. And that other one she hangs around with, that BB."

"Who did you say?"

"BB. What kind of name is that for a grown-ass man?" Mrs. Collins asked.

Black remembered the name. BB was the fourth member of the commission. The one that disappeared after Cash Money and K Murder got killed by Mylo's hit team. "I think you're right, Mrs. Collins," he said.

"I'm not sure if she'll even talk to you."

Black stood up. "She'll talk to me."

Chapter Thirty-five

After leaving Mrs. Collins's house, Black had an idea about what he thought was going on. He thought about CeeCee. Before him, she had always been a baller's woman. He thought that she too had reverted to what she knew. He left there thinking, hoping really, that Leon had her wrong, and focused his attention on finding Shy.

"We going to meet Jap at Doc's?"

"Yes," Black said. "Is there anything else going on I should know about?"

"I been meaning to ask you since you got here. Do you have Nick and Monika and them doing something for you?"

"No, why?"

"Ms. Robinson made the drive out to Rockland just to ask me if I'd seen him. Nick, Monika, Travis, and Jackie are gone."

"Gone, gone where?"

"I don't know. He didn't tell her where he was going, and she hadn't heard from him in days. Bottom line, she's worried."

"He didn't tell you either?"

"He didn't say anything to me about it."

"That group could be anywhere in the world, doing who knows what. But if she drove all the way out to Rockland it might be something. When we finish with Jap at Doc's, roll by J.R.'s and see if she's there," Black said, and Bobby headed for Doc's.

When they got to Doc's Jap was waiting. Black told Doc that he was going to use his office. "You find her?"

"No, nobody has seen Shy. But I did find Jack."

"Where did you find him?"

"He's hold up at an old girlfriend's apartment. From what I hear, he was involved in a shootout; took one in the leg, one to the gut, and a grazing to the head. He lost a lot of blood, so he's been out of it."

"Did you talk to him?"

"No, like I said, he's out of it. What little I got I dragged out of the girlfriend."

"And she couldn't tell you if Shy was part of this shootout?"

"She said she's never even heard of Shy."

"Thanks, Jap. Now there are two other niggas I want you to run down."

"Who?"

"One calls himself Blunt and the other is BB."

"Blunt I know. He shouldn't be too hard to find. And BB, the one from the old commission?"

"That's him."

"Might be a little tougher, but meet me back here in two hours and I'll let you know what or who I find," Jap said and headed for the door.

"I could use a drink," Bobby said.

"Make it to go. I wanna talk to Ms. Robinson and then roll by the hotel again."

When Black and Bobby arrived at J.R.'s, instead of asking for Rain, they went to the bar and got a drink before making their way toward the offices. If Rain were there, she'd be in her office. They got to the back and were met by two men. "Rain Robinson; she here?" Black asked.

"Who you think you talking to like that?" he said, and Black looked at him like he was stupid. Just then, Rose walked up.

"Mr. Black, Mr. Ray," Rose said. "How are you gentlemen tonight?"

"I'm doing fine, Rose. But I think you need to put your boy here in check. I was about to shoot him," Bobby said.

Rose looked at her security. "I will vouch for these two gentlemen, Willis," Rose said, and Bobby laughed.

"But Rain said she don't wanna see nobody," Willis said.

"What you talking about, Willis?" Bobby laughed.

"I don't have time for this. Get this clown out of my way," Black said.

"But Rain said—" Willis began, but Rose cut him off.

"Rain works for these gentlemen. I'm sure she'll see them."

Bobby got in Willis's face. "You do understand what that means, *Willis*. It means you work for me, too, and you're fired. Pick up your last check on the way out," he said and pushed Willis out of the way; and he and Black went in the back that led to Rain's office.

"But, Rose?" Willis said as Rose passed him.

"I'll meet you in the office when I'm done with them. But yeah, you're fired."

"You really want me to fire him, Bobby? Nigga got five kids to feed," Rose said.

"No. Give him some time off to learn to think before he opens his mouth and that when he does, to know who it is he's talking to before he does," Bobby told Rose.

Rain had gotten to the club earlier in the evening. She had nothing else to do so she came up to J.R.'s hoping that it would change her mood. It didn't. She still wanted to, needed to, know where Nick was. So after having a couple of shots of Patrón at the bar, Rain went to her office and had told the now unemployed Willis that she didn't want to see anybody.

When Rain heard the knock at the door, she threw her glass at it.

"I told you that I didn't want to be bothered!" Rain yelled without looking at her monitor.

"Rain, it's me Rose. I have Mike Black and Bobby Ray with me."

Rain looked up and saw them standing there. She turned off the big screen and buzzed them in.

"Am I interrupting something, Ms. Robinson?" Black asked and followed Rose and Bobby into the office.

"No, Mr. Black, not at all. Come in and make yourselves comfortable. Can I get you a drink?"

Bobby looked at the broken glass on the floor. "I'll have whatever you're drinking. Looks like you wasted some of that last one."

"What about you, Mr. Black?"

"I'm fine, Ms. Robinson. I ain't planning on being here that long," Black said and glanced at Bobby.

Rain walked over to the bar and poured two shots of Patrón for her and Bobby. "What can I do for you, Rose?"

"I was just passing by the office when I saw Willis giving them a hard time."

"Fire his ass, Rose. Dumb-ass mutha fucka. I never want to see his face up in here no more, understand?"

Rose looked at Bobby. "You heard what the woman said."

Rose left the office and Rain turned to Bobby. "What was that about?"

"I fired him too, but I told Rose to back off and just give him some time in the street for being disrespectful."

"No, Bobby, he's a fuckup that needs to go. Putting his ass on that door was his last chance to have a job working for me. I figured how can he fuck up just standing there. I hate a dumb-ass mutha fucka." Rain paused. "What can I do for you two?"

"Bobby says that you were worried because you haven't heard from Nick in a couple of days. I know this is not what you want to hear, but they are not working on anything for me," Black said. "That crew could be anywhere in the world, doing all kinds of shit. I wouldn't worry too much about it. Both Nick and Monika can take care of themselves."

"I know, I just feel left out, but I'll be all right," Rain said, and Black and Bobby stood up. "Where y'all going?" she wanted to know.

"You know a guy goes by the name Blunt? And another named BB?"

"Shit yeah, I know both them niggas. Y'all gonna let me ride with y'all?"

"Get your guns and let's go," Black said and headed for the door.

Chapter Thirty-six

As they were coming out of J.R.'s, Rain spotted somebody she knew. "That's Nando over there? He used to be one of BB's old crew."

"He don't seem that happy to see you, Ms. Robinson," Black replied.

"Hey, Nando!" Rain yelled. Nando looked at Rain and started running.

"He's running," Black said.

"Why is he running?" Bobby asked.

"'Cause I told him that I would cut his dick off next time I saw him," Rain said and took off running after Nando. Bobby went for his car and drove after them. Rain caught up with him just as Nando made it to his car. "Where you going, Nando?" Rain asked.

"Nowhere," Nando said as Bobby pulled up and got out of the car.

Rain pulled a knife out of her bag. "Tell me what I wanna know and I won't cut your little dick off."

"What do you wanna know?"

"Where is BB?" Rain demanded to know.

"What's in it for me?" Nando asked, and with that Black pulled him up from the ground and punched him in the stomach. Nando fell to his knees.

"If you don't tell her what she wants to know and I mean right fuckin' now, I will beat you senseless before I kill you," Black said and slammed Nando face first into the car door. "So now you know what's in it for you. Tell her what she wants to know, and I won't kill you." Black slammed his head into the door again and Rain started kicking him.

"All right, all right, Rain. He's with Dex and Lightman. They're making the rounds to all their spots."

Rain kicked him again and got in his face. "That shit don't fuckin' help me," she yelled, and Black slammed his face into the door again.

Bobby leaned over Nando. "Look, Nando is it? I think you better tell these two something before you end up dickless."

"Crazy Horse Cabaret!" Nando yelled. "Dex got a bitch that dances there."

Rain kicked him again. "Don't call her no bitch."

Black slammed his face into the door again and again.

"We better find them niggas there or I'll be back, and you'll be dickless!" Rain screamed, and then her and Black walked away laughing. They got in the car with Bobby and he drove them downtown to Lexington Avenue to see if Shy had returned to the Radisson.

They went up to her room and Black knocked on the door and waited to see if she would answer. Much to his surprise, the door swung open and there stood Shy, dressed in her kick-a-mutha-fuckas-ass leather with a gun in her waist. Thinking that it could only be Jack at her door, Shy swung it open.

"Where have you been?" she asked before she realized who was standing there.

"I've been looking for you," Black said.

"Oh ... hello, Michael. What are you doing here?"

"Hello, Cassandra. And like I said, I've been looking for you."

"Hey, Bobby," Shy said, and she gave Bobby a big hug.

"Hey, Shy."

"Cassandra, this is Ms. Robinson."

"Mrs. Black, it is an honor to finally meet you," Rain said.

"Nice to meet you too," Shy said.

"Give us a minute," Black said to Bobby and Rain.

"We'll be in the car," Bobby said. "Come on, *Ms. Robinson.*"

"Don't you start with that shit too, Bobby," Rain said as she and Bobby walked down the hall toward the elevator.

"That Bobby's new girlfriend?" Shy asked.

"Nick's actually."

"What's she doing with y'all?"

"She works for me."

"Doing what?"

"Ms. Robinson is my enforcer."

"Her?" Shy asked in disbelief.

"Her. Don't be fooled. Ms. Robinson is a bad bitch. So, can I come in?"

Without saying a word, Shy turned around and walked away from the door. Black followed her into the room. Shy took the gun from her waist and sat down on the bed; Black sat down next to her.

"Did I catch you at a bad time?" Black asked and picked up the gun.

"I was on my way out."

"Jack is okay. If that's where you were going."

"I hadn't heard from him and I was about to go see if I could find him. Where is he?"

"He's with some girlfriend of his. I don't know all the details, but I hear he was involved in a shootout." Black smelled the barrel of Shy's gun. "He took three shots: one to the leg, one in the gut, and a grazing to the head. He's lost a lot of blood, so he's been out, which is probably why you haven't heard from him."

"But he's gonna be all right, right?"

"I didn't see or talk to him. So I don't know. But what I would like to know is, were you involved in this shootout?"

Shy dropped her head. "Yes, I was there."

"Were you hurt?"

"No, Michael. I managed to get away without getting shot this time."

"What were you doing there, Cassandra? Did you decide to get back in the game?"

"No ... I guess kinda."

"What's that supposed to mean?"

"At first I was just putting Jack on to somebody he could do business with. Then I thought I could just be ... you know ... adviser and counselor, with no direct involvement. But it's a funny thing about this thing, it seems to pull you close and before you know it, you're in."

"I understand."

"Do you really, Michael?"

"Sure I do."

"Then you're not mad at me, right?"

"Wrong. I'm mad as hell with you. What were you thinking? What went wrong?"

"I'm gonna assume that you've already talked to Angelo."

"Yeah, I did talk to Angee. He gave you somebody to do business with; I get all that, but what were you doing there? Jack can't handle a buy without you?"

"It wasn't like that. I was trying to get Jack to tighten up on some things." Shy decided not to tell Black that Jack had disobeyed her orders and that was what prompted her to ride along on the deal. "But when we get there it ain't Nico Dees, it's some other guys."

"That's because Nico Dees got killed two weeks ago."

"Now that makes sense. Anyway, I had a bad feeling about them, so I started to back off, but they started shooting."

"How many people did you lose?"

"Three, and Jack got shot," Shy said sadly.

Black shook his head. "What were you thinking? Is this what you want? Is this what you want to do with your life? What about Michelle? What about me? I love you."

"I love you too. And no, this is not what I want. I'm sure of that now." Shy stood up and walked to the window. "If I wasn't sure, that night convinced me." Black got up and walked over to her. He put his arm around her. "Even though I managed to get outta there without getting shot this time, I still thought about dying. I thought about being on the island. I was sure that I was going to die alone there and now I have a second chance to be with you and for us to raise our daughter; watch her grow up. And what am I doing? I'm doing everything I can to put myself in a position to die in the street. That's not what I really want."

"Then you need to tell me just what it is that you do want, Cassandra. I think I deserve that much."

"I wanna be with you, Michael."

"Then come home."

"Home where?"

"To my house in Nassau."

Shy looked at him like he had called her everything but a child of God. "Michael, I am sure that it is a wonderful house, but I wouldn't be caught dead in that house."

"Why?" Black asked and then he thought about it. "Never mind, I see your point."

"Good. I didn't really feel like explaining that to you. But I tell you what I will do; I will go to *our house* in Freeport and wait for you."

"Fair enough. You go down there, and I will have M bring you the kids."

"What kids?"

214

"I'm keeping Easy."

Shy smiled. "What's his mama gonna say about that?"

"Fuck her. She ain't the slightest bit interested in that boy. He's mine and I'm keeping him."

"No."

"No?"

"No, he's ours and we're keeping him."

Chapter Thirty-seven

"Where you going now?" Shy asked when Black started for the door. After the talk they had just had, she was expecting something a little different.

"Do you trust me?" Black asked, not wanting to tell Shy that he was leaving her to look for CeeCee.

"Yes, Michael, I trust you ... always."

"Just know that I gotta go do this." Black took her in his arms. "Know that I love you more than I can find words to express. You saying that you're ready to come be with us has made me the happiest man alive. And I want to get started on rebuilding our lives, but I gotta go do this."

Shy kissed him. "I understand. Can you at least tell me how long you'll be?"

"No, I can't. But I want you outta here tonight. There is a charter plane at Kennedy. He'll take you to Freeport."

"Okay, Michael. I will see you when you get there."

Black kissed Shy and left the room. The smile on his face told the entire story. He had to get his game face on before he got in the car with Bobby and Rain.

"You and the Mrs. got shit worked out?" Bobby asked.

"Yeah, she's gonna leave tonight and meet me in Freeport."

"So where we going now?"

"Back uptown to the Crazy Horse. Let's see if Ms. Robinson is gonna have to cut that nigga's dick off or not," Black said, and Rain pulled out her knife to show she was ready. But he was as good as his word. BB, Dex and Lightman were outside the Crazy Horse, leaning against a car when Black got out of Bobby's car.

"Oh shit," BB said when he saw Black coming.

"What?" Lightman asked.

"Here comes Black."

"You ain't scared of this nigga, are you?" Lightman asked.

"Yeah, he is," Dex said. "You want me to handle him?"

"No," BB said, "I got this."

Black walked right up to him. "BB, right?"

"Yeah."

"Let me holla at you for a minute."

After BB walked away with Black, Bobby and Rain stepped up. The stare down began immediately, with Dex and Lightman mean mugging, and Bobby and Rain smiling and laughing at them.

"Where's CeeCee?"

"I don't know."

"Don't lie to me."

"Look, all I know is that she said that she was rolling out with some nigga named Blunt that she wanna bring in."

"Bring in to what?"

"Our thing."

"What you mean *our thing?*"

"Our thing," BB said and pointed at Dex and Lightman.

Black grabbed BB by the shirt, spun him around, and slammed him into a car. Dex and Lightman moved, but they didn't get far before Bobby and Rain had four guns pointed at them.

"You don't want none of this, youngster. And I know he ain't about to fuck with you, Rain."

"You Rain Robinson?" Lightman asked.

"What about it?" Rain said and put the barrels of one of her guns to Lightman's head.

"Nothing. I just heard you was a bad bitch."

"You heard right. So take a good look," Rain said.

217

Black took out his gun and pressed it under BB's chin. "What, is CeeCee backing you?"

"She was. Then she flipped it and took over. Now this is her thing."

Black shook his head. "Understand this ... if anything happens to her, if she stubs her fuckin' toe, I'm gonna come back here and kill you. Are we clear?"

"Crystal," BB said, and Black let him go.

Once they were back in Bobby's car, Black told them what BB said. "We need to find this nigga Blunt."

They rode around to a few of the spots Rain thought he might be and then Black saw somebody he and Bobby knew from the old days.

"Stop the car, Bobby," he said and got out. "Lillian!" he shouted at the top of his lungs.

Babygirl's head snapped around. She smiled and started walking toward Black. "Who is this calling me by my government name?" she said, and Knives started walking with her. "Must be a badass nigga for him to think he could get away with that shit," Babygirl said and then she rushed forward and jumped in his arms. "Hey, Mike Black," she said and kissed him on the cheek.

"What's up, Babygirl. Heard you was back in the city terrorizing niggas."

"You know me. I do what I do," Babygirl said, and then she saw Bobby. She did the same thing to him. "Somehow I knew if Black was here that you wasn't too far away, Bobby."

"You know it."

The entire time the reunion of old friends was going on, Knives kept her hands on her guns and Rain kept her eyes on Knives. She knew Babygirl and Knives and didn't trust them.

I hate sneaky bitches.

"Maybe you can help me with something," Black said.

"Anything for you, baby boy, you know that."

"I'm looking for a nigga named Blunt."

"We know him, don't we, Knives?" Babygirl said and both she and Knives laughed. "We had that nigga set up and ready. Then he backed away from us; started fuckin' with some other niggas. So you know me, I said fuck it, we'll just rob them. Didn't we, Knives?"

"But they turned out to be worse than we are. Niggas he fuckin' with now will rob him, and then they'll kill him," Knives said.

"Where can I find them?" Black asked.

"They been operating outta a spot on Bryant Avenue."

"In Hunts Point?"

"The one and only."

Inside a building on Bryant Avenue in Hunts Point, Monk was weighing his options. One of his men was dead; another was in police custody.

"And you know that niggas gonna talk."

It was time to cut his losses and head back to Cleveland. But a little traveling money wouldn't hurt. Monk looked at his watch and knew that this evening's mark would be there soon.

Blunt parked outside the building. "Remind me again, what are we here for?" CeeCee asked.

"I'm here to see what kind of price this Nico Dees can offer me. You're here to keep me company, Cami."

"You need to go on and face the facts. Nobody is gonna give you a better price than me."

"Is that a fact?"

"Fact. So why don't you start this bad boy up and get me out from down here, then you can buy me a drink."

219

"I came all the way down here, Cami; the least I can do is hear what the man got to say." Blunt leaned over and kissed her on the cheek. "Stay in the car, I won't be long and then we can go have that drink."

CeeCee watched as Blunt got out, walked toward the building, and went inside. It was then that she realized that he had taken the keys and it would get hot and stuffy in that car pretty quick. She had just gotten her hair done that afternoon and wasn't thinking about ruining it.

Just as a precaution, CeeCee reached in her purse and got out her gun. Then she opened the car door and got out. She put her gun on the roof of the car, and with the car door still open, CeeCee leaned against it.

Back inside the building, Blunt walked in the room with Monk. "I'm looking for Nico Dees," Blunt said.

"Well you found him," Monk said and noticed that Blunt was both alone and empty-handed. "Are you ready to do business?"

"That depends on what you talking about. You give me a price I can work with and then we can make arrangements to do business," Blunt said.

Monk and Bailey looked at each other. "So you here to talk and you ain't got no money."

It was only then that Blunt began to realize what he'd walked into. But it was too late to do anything about it now. Both Monk and Bailey raised their weapons and shot Blunt.

"Talk about that," Monk said and packed up the rest of their stuff. They would ride by the hotel and then head back to Cleveland. Once they were done, they got in their van and drove out. As they drove down the street, Monk saw CeeCee leaning on the roof of the car. He put his gun on his lap. CeeCee saw them coming and reached for her gun.

Monk pulled up alongside her. "What you looking at?" CeeCee asked.

"A dead bitch," Monk said. He raised his weapon and fired. "Drive."

He hit CeeCee with one shot to the head. She died instantly.

Chapter Thirty-eight

"He did what?" Robert shouted. He was at home for the evening, enjoying a quiet night at home with his wife and their younger children.

"After he killed the nigga she was with, Monk rolled up on her and shot her in the head. I thought you'd want to know right away."

"Yeah, yeah, thanks, Eddie," Robert said quickly; then he got careless. "You get as many people as you need, but you bring that nigga to me at the restaurant."

"Yes, sir. What about the nigga that's with him? You want him too?"

"I don't care what you do with him, just bring me Monk," Robert said and ended the call. "Fuck!" he shouted as he dialed a number.

"What's up, Pop?" Ronnie said when he answered.

"We got problems. Meet me at the restaurant as soon as you can."

Ronnie looked at the woman he was with and shook his head. "What's wrong, Pop?"

"I'll tell you when I see you, boy. Now get out that pussy and get down there."

"Yes, sir."

By the time Robert got there and went to the back, Eddie had Monk. "Evening, Mr. Monk."

"What's this about, King?" Monk demanded to know. He was surrounded by six men who all had their guns pointed at him.

Robert laughed when he saw the setup. "Six niggas, Eddie?"

"I didn't think he was gonna come quietly. And he didn't. He kicked up a little dust, but we were able to

convince him that coming with us was in his best interest,"
Eddie said, and the men laughed. That's when Robert
noticed the cuts and bruises on Monk's face.

"What about the other one?"

Eddie ran his finger across his throat. "He didn't wanna
come quietly either."

When Ronnie came rushing in, his reaction was the
same. Robert turned and went into his office. "Bring that
nigga in, Eddie."

"The rest of you hang around for a few," Ronnie said
and followed Eddie and Monk into his father's office.

"So, you gonna tell me what this is about?" Monk asked
again.

"We brought you in to do a job. You got paid and paid
well when the job was over. But here's the thing; I didn't
bring you in from Cleveland to hang around. I brought you
in from Cleveland to take your ass back to Cleveland when
the job was done."

"I saw an opportunity to make some money here, so I
stayed. Anything wrong with that?"

"Yes. Yes, there is. But since what you were doing was
working in my best interest, like a fool I let you go on and
do what you were doing. My thinking was ... far be it for me
to get in the way of somebody trying to earn a living."

"So what's the problem?"

"The problem begins when your earning a living brings
the cops to my office. Now I would have thought that when
the police killed one of your crew and arrested the other that
it would be a signal for you to take your ass back to
Cleveland. But it wasn't. Here you still are."

"We needed some traveling money," Monk said.

"Your needing traveling money may just have had the effect of bringing more heat on me from people I don't need it from."

"What he do, Pop?" Ronnie asked.

Robert signaled for Ronnie to come closer. "This nigga done fucked around and shot Mike Black's baby mama. She's dead."

Ronnie looked at Monk.

"What I do?"

Neither Robert nor Ronnie said anything to Monk.

"I knew something like this was gonna happen. That's why you went outta your way to make sure that Black wouldn't get into this. You shoulda let me drop him when he finished what we brought him here for."

"You're right, and I should have listened. Now we got Kirk on one side and Black on the other. Time to cut ties with this nigga before Black finds out who killed her, and that we brought him here."

"I agree."

"I want you to check with that girl you been playing with and find out what he knows."

"What about him?"

"Drop him."

"Yes, sir," Ronnie said and left the office.

"Mr. Monk?"

"Yeah."

"Just what is it gonna take for you to go back to Cleveland and never come back to New York?"

Monk smiled and then laughed a little. "I think fifty grand will make that happen."

"Eddie, take Mr. Monk to Ronald's office and then you take him back to Cleveland. That means you get his ticket and you get on the plane with him and take him back to Cleveland. Understand?"

"Yes, sir?"

"Good." Robert looked at Monk. "You go with Eddie and my son Ronald will take care of you."

Monk bounced up from his chair. "Pleasure doing business with you, Mr. King."

"I wish I could say the same. Eddie, get this nigga outta my sight."

Eddie escorted Monk to Ronnie's office and knocked on the door. "Come," Ronnie shouted. Eddie came in with Monk. "You gentlemen excuse the mess. I been having the office renovated," he said when Monk looked down at the drop cloth on the floor. "Have a seat, Mr. Monk." Monk sat down and Ronnie looked at Eddie. "What did Pop say to do with him?"

"Give him fifty gee's and take him back to Cleveland." Monk smiled thinking that this was working out well for him. Not only was he getting fifty grand, but a free flight back to Cleveland.

Ronnie went to his safe and counted off fifty thousand dollars, put it in an envelope and handed it to Monk. He sat there and counted it. "Thanks, King. Like I told your pops, it was a pleasure doing business with you two."

"I wish I could say the same."

Eddie laughed as Monk got up.

"What?"

"That's the same thing your pops said."

When Monk turned around to laugh with Eddie, Ronnie walked up behind him and put two in the back of his head.

"Get my money and get this trash outta here," Ronnie said. He sat down at his desk as Eddie went out and got two more men to wrap Monk up in the drop cloth and carry him out. Next thing he needed to do was find Rain to see if any of this mess had gotten back to them.

Chapter Thirty-nine

Bobby turned on Bryant Avenue and rolled slowly down the street. It was Rain who first noticed Blunt's car with the interior light on. Then she saw the open car door. Bobby slowed down.

"Pull over, Bobby," Rain said. "Something just don't seem right about this picture."

Bobby parked the car and Rain got out. She took out her gun and slowly approached the car. Black and Bobby got out and followed Rain down the street toward the car. It was dark, but the closer Rain got to the car the clearer it became. When she got to the door, Rain saw the body. She looked back at Black and Bobby.

"I got a body here," she said, and Black walked faster. "It's a woman!"

Black looked at the body and even in the dark, he knew it was CeeCee. Since it was so dark, he didn't see the wound. He felt for a pulse. CeeCee was dead. Her body was still warm so he knew that it must have just happened. CeeCee was dead because he wasn't there to protect her. He felt his legs get weak as the rush of emotions washed over him. Thoughts of the night he found the body that, at the time he thought was Shy, filled his mind. He sat down next to her body and looked at her.

"Damn, Cee, what were you doing?" he asked quietly. "What were you trying to prove? Sorry I didn't get here in time to save you."

"That her?" Bobby asked. Black didn't look up; he just nodded his head. "I'm sorry, Mike."

Rain stepped closer to Bobby. "Who is she?"

"That's his son's mother."

Rain looked at Black sitting there and didn't know what to say. "I'm sorry," she said, and a tear rolled down her cheek. She quickly wiped it away.

He sat there for a while staring at CeeCee, before he finally looked up at Bobby and Rain. "Get that gun off the roof of the car, Ms. Robinson and get rid of it. Then you wipe the car down anywhere you think she might have touched."

"On it," Rain said and rushed away, happy to be doing something other than just standing there looking at the body.

"Bobby, find a phone and call Billy. He's probably still at the parlor. Tell him to send a wagon to get her body."

"Right." Bobby went to find a phone. He passed by a building with the door open. He took out his gun and went toward the building. As he got closer, he could see what looked like a body just outside the door. He walked up on the body slowly; he could see a trail of blood. It looked like he crawled and lived long enough to make it outside.

Bobby checked for a pulse and found none. Since he was looking for a phone, Bobby checked his pockets and found Blunt's phone. After he called Billy, Bobby left the building.

"Wagon is on its way," Bobby said when he got back to Black. "Found another body in that building over there." Bobby pointed to the building. "Probably this Blunt guy she came here with," he said, but Black didn't say anything or even look up. He just stared at CeeCee's body.

It was thirty minutes later when the wagon arrived. The driver and his assistant got out the stretcher. Black picked up CeeCee's body and placed it on the stretcher. It was only then that he saw the bullet wound in her forehead. He took a step back and allowed the men to do their work. He stood silently and watched as they placed CeeCee's body in the wagon and drove off.

I should have been here. Sorry I wasn't here in time, he thought and remembered thinking those same thoughts and feeling those same feelings the night he found the body he thought was Shy. He couldn't help but wonder had CeeCee just paid the price for his beloved Cassandra being alive.

Black walked back to Bobby's car where he and Rain were waiting. "I'm sorry, Black," Rain said quickly.

"I am too, Mike. Anything you need, just tell me," Bobby said.

"Take me to her mother's house."

"You want to do that now?"

Black turned to Bobby and Bobby saw the rage in his eyes. "Yeah, Bobby, I fuckin' wanna go there now!" he yelled and got in the car.

Rain and Bobby got in and they made the drive back to Mrs. Collins house. Bobby parked the car. Black handed Bobby his guns.

"Wait here."

He got out and walked quietly to the door, and rang the bell. "Who is it?"

"It's Michael, Mrs. Collins."

She opened the door. "What's wrong?" She knew by the hour of his visit and the look on his face that something was definitely wrong.

"Can I come in?"

"What's wrong?" Mrs. Collins said as she back slowly away from the door. Even though he hadn't said it, deep inside she already knew. She closed the door and grabbed his arm. "You tell me what's wrong, Michael."

"I'm sorry." Black turned around slowly and looked at Mrs. Collins as tears began to roll down her cheeks. "I'm sorry to tell you that somebody shot CeeCee. She's dead," he said and held out his arms. As her tears flowed hard, Mrs. Collins stepped into his arms and he held her.

"You sure she's gone, Michael. Ain't no mistake, is it? You know they make those kinds of mistakes all the time," she said quickly and tearfully.

"No mistake, she's gone. I'm sorry that I didn't get there in time to save her," Black said and held her tighter. Each could feel the other's pain. "I couldn't save her."

Mrs. Collins broke their embrace and wiped away her tears. "Do you know what happened to her?"

"No, not yet. But I promise you that I will find out who did this, and I will kill them."

Mrs. Collins dropped her head and walked into her living room. She sat on the couch and looked at Black. "Don't you think there's been enough killing done already?" she asked him. "Is your killing whoever did this going to bring Cameisha back?"

"No, it won't." He came and sat next to her. She took his hand.

"I know you're hurting right now. I can feel it. So am I. I lost my only child tonight and no mother ever wants to bury their child. But neither one of us sent Cameisha in them streets, Michael. That's a choice she made. She should have been here taking care of the beautiful baby boy that she brought into this world."

"I understand all that but—" Black began, but she put her finger over his lips.

"There is no but here, Michael. There are only the facts; Cameisha is with the Father now and there is nothing you or I can do to change that." Mrs. Collins began to cry again. Black held her and she cried on his shoulder. Then she quickly wiped away her tears. "I need to go claim the body."

"I've got her body at the funeral home I own."

"Thank you, Michael," she said and stood up. Black stood up and she walked him to the door. "Now you promise me, Michael ... promise me that you're not gonna go around killing the people that did this. I put it in the hands of the Lord. Dearly beloved, avenge not yourselves, but *rather* give place unto wrath; for it is written, Vengeance *is* mine; I will repay, saith the Lord," Mrs. Collins said quoting from the King James Version of the Bible.

"I promise."

"I mean it now, Michael," she said and opened the door. Before he walked out Mrs. Collins hugged him.

Black walked to the car and got in. "Where to now?" Bobby asked and handed Black back his guns.

"Let's go find BB and kill him," Black said and put one in the chamber of each gun.

"That's what I'm talking about," Rain said and checked her weapons.

Bobby started up the car and drove on. "Explain to me again, why we killing this nigga?"

"'Cause I promised him I would," Black said.

"Yeah, but why?"

"'Cause he brought her in."

"If he didn't bring her in, that guy Blunt would have."

"No. She was trying to bring him into their thing. And besides, he's already dead."

"Okay. All I'm saying is that you need to calm down and think this thing through. You do shit when you're mad; you end up making stupid mistakes," Bobby advised.

"I am calm, Bobby, but I tell you what," Black said and leaned close to Bobby. He whispered something to him, and Bobby laughed.

"Rain."

"Yeah."

"I want you to handle killing BB."

"No problem. Y'all gonna roll with me or I need to get my people?"

"We're with you, Ms. Robinson," Black said.

"Cool. Roll by the Crazy Horse; see if they still there. But if you see a store on the way, stop. I need to pick up something." On the way back to the Crazy Horse, Bobby stopped at a store and Rain went in. "Okay, let's go," she said when she came out.

When they got back to the Crazy Horse, Black and Bobby started to get out.

"No, y'all stay here. I'ma go inside and see if they still in there. You two attract too much attention."

Rain went in the club and saw that BB, Dex and Lightman were still inside. They were at a table near the back, surrounded by dancers and dropping money like it was water. Rain went back to the car.

"They in there. At a table near the back."

"So how you wanna do this?" Bobby asked.

Rain reached in the bag she came out of the store with. "Here, y'all put them on." She handed Bobby a pair of stockings. "We rush the door. I got Dex; Bobby, you take Lightman; Black, BB is yours. One to the chest, one to the dome, and we outta there."

"Sounds like a plan to me, Bob," Black said and put on his mask.

When Bobby and Rain were ready, they got out and rushed the door. Their entrance caused a bit of a commotion. It got BB's attention. He saw three people in masks running toward the table. Knowing that Black promised to kill him and never being one to take any chances, BB got up and headed for the back door.

Dex and Lightman watched BB run off. By the time they looked around, Bobby and Rain were on top of them. As Black ran after BB, Bobby and Rain fired twice. One shot a piece to the chest and then one shot a piece to the head. Then they followed Black out the back door.

"I'll stay on Black; you get the car," Rain yelled to Bobby and he headed in that direction.

BB ran around the building and made it to the street, and headed for his car. He looked back and saw the masked man running behind him. He got off a couple of shots as he ran, but he missed. Once he made it to the car, he fumbled for his keys, which gave Black a chance to catch up. Black knocked the keys out of BB's hand with one gun and put the other to his chest. Black took off his mask because he wanted BB to see his face when he died.

"Time to die," he said and pulled the trigger. Then he took a step back and fired one shot to the head as Rain ran up. She took off her mask and put one in his chest.

"Where's Bobby?" Black asked.

"He went for the car."

"Let's find him and get outta here," Black said and walked off with Rain.

Chapter Forty

"Happy now?" Bobby asked when Black and Rain got in the car with him.

"Yeah, Bobby, as a matter of fact I am."

"Good. But that don't get us no closer to finding out who actually killed CeeCee and this other nigga. You know that, right?"

"I know. So take me back to where we saw Babygirl. See what else she can tell us."

"See, now you're making sense," Bobby said and drove on.

They searched for Babygirl and Knives for the rest of the night, but they were nowhere to be found. The next day they were back in the streets looking for them. It took the rest of the day, but they finally found them.

"Did you find what you were looking for last night, baby boy?" Babygirl said to Black.

"I did, but now I need to know something else from you, Babygirl."

"See, you gonna find that I am the indispensable woman and that you gotta have me around you all the time," Babygirl said and looked at Rain.

"Maybe. But for the time being I just need to know who was that your boy Blunt was going to see?"

"What the fuck was his name? Help me out here, Knives," Babygirl said and turned to her partner in crime.

"Guy's name is Monk. He's outta Cleveland," Knives said.

When Rain heard the name Monk, she leaned toward Black. "I need to tell you something," she said.

"Go ahead."

"Not in front of these dollar-store bitches," Rain said and started walking to the car. Bobby and Black looked at each other.

Black stepped quickly to catch up with Rain. "I'll get with you, Babygirl," he said without looking back.

Bobby laughed. "I guess I'll see you dollar-store bitches later," he said and followed Rain to the car

"Fuck you, Bobby," Babygirl said.

Bobby turned around, but kept walking. "Not this time but next time, you can give me some of that fat-ass pussy. But I gotta go now. There's killing to be done," he said and got in his car.

"Now," Black began, "what you need to tell me that you couldn't say in front of them?"

"I was at Robert and Ronnie King's restaurant and Ronnie introduced me to Monk."

"What were you doing there?" Black asked.

"Me and Ronnie used to date back in the day. But let me tell you, I was there another night when Kirk showed up there and I heard Robert tell Ronnie that he needs to find Monk and shut him down."

"Now it makes sense," Bobby said.

"What's that?" Black asked.

"Do you remember Wanda telling you that Robert King wanted to meet with you?"

"Yeah, and I told Wanda that I didn't want to or need to meet with him."

"You told her to talk to me and see if I'd meet with him," Bobby said. "Well me, Nick and Wanda met with him."

"What did you take Wanda for?"

"Because like it or not, Mike, Wanda is a part of this family. And like it or not, she does come in handy at meetings like that because she can be such a ruthless mutha fucka when she needs to be," Bobby said and looked at Rain. "And on top of that, you put me in charge of this side of the house and I felt like she needed to be there."

"You're right on all three counts, Bob, but you know that ain't the point. But it is your show, and I'm not going to tell you how to run it," Black said.

When Rain heard all that, she felt bad because Nick was telling the truth. He was at a meeting with Bobby, and Wanda was there against Black's ban. But there was still one more thing that she needed to know.

"Since I backed Leon against Rico, King wanted to be sure that we didn't have any plans of getting back in with Leon. After that meeting a lot of drug dealers started turning up dead," Bobby said. "They imported this nigga Monk from Cleveland to kill off the competition, and then him and Ronnie become the major players in the game because ain't nobody left."

"How come you two are just telling me this now?"

"Honestly, Mike, I didn't connect the two," Bobby said.

"Neither did I," Rain agreed.

"What you wanna do now, Mike?" Bobby asked.

"I think we need to pay the King's a visit," Black said as Bobby headed in that direction.

"Was Ronnie at that meeting, Bobby?"

"He was. Then he left and came back when we were getting ready to wrap up," Bobby said. "Why?"

"There was a lot more going on than either of us realized," Rain said.

Now she knew that Ronnie was playing her. He knew exactly where Nick was. That's why he drove her over there so she could see Nick's car and think the worst. For that, Ronnie would have to pay.

ROY GLENN

Count on it.

Chapter Forty-one

"We got him!" Bautista shouted to nobody in particular.

She had just reviewed the transcript of the wiretap on Robert King's home phone. She rushed to get to the actual recording. Once she had it, she went to find Kirk.

"What you got, Marita?" Kirk said, and she was surprised that he called her by her first name. Kirk always called her Bautista or Detective.

"We got him, partner. We got Robert King on the wire," Bautista said as she cued up the recording and handed Kirk the transcript. "Listen to this."

Sorry to bother you at home, sir, but I thought you'd want to hear this right away.

What's that, Eddie?

Monk just did two more people. One of them was a woman. Mike Black's son's mother.

He did what?

After he killed the nigga she was with, Monk rolled up on her and shot her in the head. I thought you'd want to know right away.

Yeah, yeah, thanks, Eddie. You get as many people as you need, but you bring that nigga to me at the restaurant.

Yes, sir. What about the nigga that's with him, you want him too?

I don't care what you do with him, just bring me Monk.

"Then he called his son," Bautista said excitedly.

What's up, Pop?

We got problems. Meet me at the restaurant as soon as you can.

What's wrong, Pop?

I'll tell you when I see you, boy. Now get out that pussy and get down there.

Yes, sir.

Bautista looked at Kirk. "What's wrong?"

Kirk looked at Bautista and played the recording again while he read the transcript. "Nothing's wrong. We got King dead-on, but matters may have just gotten worse. Come on. Let's get this to the captain." Kirk walked away quickly, and Bautista struggled to catch up.

"How did things get worse?" she asked as they got to the captain's office.

Kirk turned and looked at Bautista. "The woman Monk shot was Mike Black's son's mother. I'm just afraid of what Black will do when he hears about it."

"Good thing he's in Nassau."

"Yeah."

Kirk and Bautista went in and let their captain hear what they had. Once he heard it, he called the assistant district attorney. She wanted to hear the recording for herself. Once she heard it she agreed it was enough to get an arrest warrant, and got a judge to issue a warrant for the arrest of Robert and Ronald King.

Armed with a warrant, Kirk and Bautista headed straight for the King's restaurant. "Do you think we need backup?" Bautista asked.

"I don't think the old man will give us any trouble. But the son, on the other hand, he may not want to go quietly. So just to be on the safe side, have one unit back us up and another on standby."

When they arrived at the restaurant, the detectives walked in like they owned the place. "Hey, you can't go back there," one of the employees, shouted. But Kirk was not fazed. He walked into Robert's office without bothering to knock.

"The sign on the door says private," Robert said.

"Robert King. I have a warrant for your arrest," Bautista said.

"On what charge?"

"Conspiracy to commit murder."

Kirk smiled at Robert. "Stand up." While Kirk put the cuffs on him, he got in Robert's ear. "Told you I'd get you."

"You ain't got nothing on me, Kirk. I'll be out in time for dinner," Robert said, and Kirk walked him out.

As Kirk was walking Robert King out, Black, Bobby, and Rain arrived at the restaurant.

"Police on scene," Bobby said.

"That is never a good thing," Rain commented.

"Park over there," Black said and pointed to a spot across the street from the restaurant. They got out of the car in time to see Kirk and Bautista perp-walking Robert to a car.

When Kirk saw Black, he turned Robert over to their uniformed backup. "Come on, Detective. There are some people you need to meet." Bautista walked across the street with Kirk thinking, *We are back to Detective just that quick.*

"Here comes Kirk." Bobby laughed.

"I see him," Black said.

"He told me to stay away from them 'cause he was gonna take them down," Rain said.

"Kirk don't say shit he don't mean," Black said. "Detective. And who is the lovely lady?"

"My new partner, Detective Bautista. Detective, this is Mike Black, Bobby Ray, and you've already met Ms. Robinson."

Bautista nodded her head.

Kirk smiled a satisfied smile at Black. "I got here first."

"What do you mean, Detective?"

"You and I both know why you're here, but I got here first," Kirk said with his smile broadening. "Walk with me, Black," he said, leaving Bautista with Rain and Bobby. "I'm sorry about your son's mother."

"Thank you."

"Tell me what you know."

"We on or off the record?"

"Strictly off the record."

"You got here first, you go first," Black said.

"Fair enough. Somebody has been killing drug dealers. I figured it was the type of thing that King would do, only he's too smart for him or his son to do the work personally. So, they bring in Monk from Cleveland. But Monk got out of their control and they had to do something about him. Your turn."

"I heard the she had been rolling with the wrong people. I came up here to talk to her, but I was too late. I heard that the guy she was with was meeting with Monk. She was dead when I got there."

"Where was the meeting?"

"Warehouse on Bryant Avenue."

"That's why I haven't heard about it. You know where Monk is?"

"No."

"I need to get to him first too, don't I?" Kirk asked.

"If I said yes, that would be like admitting that I planned on killing him. Now you answer a question for me."

"What's that?"

"Ronnie King; he in custody too?"

"No, but we have warrants for both him and Monk, so please give some thought to letting us arrest them so they can stand trial."

"I'll give it some thought," Black said and extended his hand to Kirk. They shook hands and went their separate ways.

"What was that about?" Bobby asked when Black got in the car with him and Rain.

"He wants me to consider leaving Monk and Ronnie to the police."

"Are you?" Bobby asked.

Black just looked at Bobby and then turned to Rain.

"Make finding Monk your top priority, Ms. Robinson. Put Jap on it."

"On it."

"Now, where does Ronnie live?"

"I don't know where he lives."

"You don't?" Bobby questioned.

"We wasn't like that, Bobby. But if he knows the police are after him, I might know where he's hiding." Rain told Bobby where to go and they were on their way. When they got there, Black and Bobby started to get out. "Better if I go alone," she told them.

"I was about to ask if you thought you could handle him alone, but I know you can," Black said to her as she got out of the car.

"Ronnie's a pussy. All talk. If he's in there what do you want me to do with him?"

"End him," Black said.

"That's what I'm talking about," Rain said and walked down the street; and then she went down an alley. The further she went, the more she knew that she was in the right place. When Rain saw that there an old metal trashcan knocked over on its side she was sure of it. She picked up the trashcan and climbed up. Then Rain reached for the ladder and pulled it down enough for her to climb up. Once she got to the fire escape, Rain went up to the fourth floor, opened the window, and went inside. Rain walked up to a door and knocked.

"Open the door, Ronnie. I know you in there!"

"Who that?"

"Rain. Open the door, nigga." Ronnie opened the door and held it open for her to come in. "I knew you was here," Rain said and walked in behind Ronnie.

"Question is, what you doing here?"

"I came to kill you," Rain said.

She took out her gun and shot Ronnie twice in the back of the head. Then she took some plastic gloves out of her back pocket and searched the place. Rain found twenty thousand dollars in cash. She took the money, got the keys out of his pocket, and left the way she came. She thought about setting the building on fire, but since other people might also be squatting in the abandoned building, she changed her mind and went back to the car.

"Was he in there?" Bobby asked.

"He was. Drive around the area, Bobby. I wanna see if I can find something," Rain said. Bobby drove around until Rain saw Ronnie's Mercedes. "Let me out here."

"Where you going?" Black asked.

"I'm gonna take that Mercedes to the chop shop. Why don't you pick me up there; then we'll go by J.R.'s and I'll buy you a drink."

Chapter Forty-two

Halfway around the world, the team had begun the final phase of their mission. They arrived in Abuja, the capital city of Nigeria, located in the center of Nigeria, within the Federal Capital Territory. The name Nigeria was taken from the Niger River, which runs through the country. The British colonized Nigeria in the late nineteenth and early twentieth century, setting up administrative structures and law, while recognizing traditional chiefs. Nigeria became independent again in 1960. Abuja is a planned city, built in the 1980s and officially became Nigeria's capital in December 1991, replacing Lagos, which is still the country's most populous city.

Nigeria has one of the fastest growing telecommunications markets in the world; major emerging market operators are basing their largest and most profitable centers in Abuja. One of those operators is Zamfara Communications, which intelligence believes is a front for terrorist groups.

For this phase of the mission, the team had adopted the names of constellations. Nick was Orion, Monika was Pegasus, Jackie was Andromeda, Travis was Chamaeleon, and Xavier chose Sextans. "Why?" Monika wanted to know.

"Because it's best seen in April at 9:00 P.M. and that is the month and time I was born," Xavier answered. The fact that the standard abbreviation for Sextans was Sex wasn't lost on him.

At 10 o'clock in the morning, a maintenance truck driven by Xavier stopped at the main gate. Xavier handed the guard his ID.

"Where's Namadi today?" the guard asked.

"Called in sick this morning," Xavier said. Namadi had the misfortune of drinking with Monika at a bar the night before. She drugged him; then stole his truck and ID. Xavier's picture was then placed on it over Namadi's. After the gate guard thoroughly checked the truck, he passed Xavier through.

"I'm in Andromeda."

"Acknowledged, Sextans," Jackie said.

Getting through the gate was the easy part. Access to the sensitive areas of the main building was controlled by a security database. "Proceeding as planned," Xavier said.

He drove the truck around to the loading dock, got out, and got his toolbox. Xavier waved casually to the guard and went inside. When he got to the communications room, Xavier entered the code and went in. "Located server." As quickly as he could, Xavier connected a portable drive to the system. "Sextans to Andromeda."

"Go ahead."

"Connected."

"Stand by. Andromeda to Chamaeleon, we have access."

"Stand by Andromeda," Travis said. He was in a hotel room not far away from the Zamfara Communications grounds. Travis went to work. "Andromeda, we now have control of the cameras and the elevators. Downloading security file. Stand by."

"Standing by."

"Download complete," Travis said.

"Acknowledged. Proceeding to phase two."

While Xavier headed back to his truck, Nick and Monika approached the main gate. "Dawud Iskandar and associate to see Abd-Al-Qadir," Nick said to the gate guard.

The guard took a quick look inside the vehicle, had them open the trunk, and then he passed them through the gate.

"Orion to Andromeda. Pegasus and I are in. Proceeding as planned," Nick said.

"Acknowledged," Jackie said as she stopped to pick up Xavier. While she drove, he took off the maintenance coveralls he was wearing. He got the case with his rifle and Jackie dropped him off at a building with a clear view of the Zamfra Communications grounds.

He went to the space that had been rented for them, and Xavier got set up. "Sextans to Andromeda; in position and standing by."

"Acknowledged."

Inside the building, Nick approached the security desk and handed the guard his ID. The guard ran the ID through his scanner and an image slowly appeared on the screen identifying Nick as Dawud Iskandar. The guard handed Nick back the ID and passed Nick through to the metal detector. He put the case containing the guidance system on the conveyor belt. Once it was cleared, Nick picked up the case and headed to the office of Abd-Al-Qadir. "Orion to Andromeda; proceeding to objective. I'll keep this line open."

"Acknowledged."

Shortly thereafter, Monika approached the desk and presented her ID. It identified her as Helon Saro Wiwa, a technology expert from nearby Cameroon, with an appointment to see the IT director. Security scanned her ID and she was passed through without incident. "Pegasus to Andromeda; proceeding to objective," Monika said and went toward the elevator.

"Acknowledged."

With Travis in control of the elevators, when she arrived one opened in front of her. Monika took the elevator to the sixth floor where the server was located. When she arrived at the server room, Monika entered the access code and went inside. She immediately connected her tablet to the main server. "Pegasus to Chamaeleon, you should have access to the data," Monika said.

"Acknowledged, uploading data. Stand by." Travis uploaded all the data from the server. "Upload complete."

"Proceeding to phase three, Andromeda," Monika said. She left the server room and proceeded to the elevator, which Travis had waiting for her. Monika got off in the basement.

"The word is go, Orion," Jackie advised.

Nick knocked on the office door of Abd-Al-Qadir. "Entrer," he said in French. "C'est bon enfin vous rencontrer dans la personne après avoir communiqué par courrier électronique pour tant de mois."

"J'ai attendu avec impatience cette réunion, monsieur. Vous m'honorez en parlant en français," Nick replied quickly.

"Parlez-vous l'anglais?"

"Yes," Nick said.

"I am more comfortable speaking English. My French is a little rusty."

"You speak it quite well," Nick said, and was glad that he did because his French was more than a little rusty.

While Nick made small talk with Al-Qadir, Monika went around the basement of the building planting explosives that she would detonate manually at the appropriate time.

"Phase three complete, Andromeda. Standing by," Monika advised.

When Nick heard that phase three was complete, he prepared to do business. "Shall we get down to business?"

"Yes, by all means. Is that it?" Al-Qadir asked and pointed to the case.

"It most certainly is, sir. Would you care to inspect it?"

"Of course."

Nick placed the case on the desk in front of Al-Qadir and he carefully examined the guidance system. Once Al-Qadir was satisfied that the item was genuine, Nick closed the case.

Al-Qadir sat down and turned to his computer and accessed his account; and then turned the computer toward Nick. "Please, enter the account that you wish your payment transferred to."

Nick leaned over the desk and entered the account number supplied by Colonel Mathis. "Transfer complete," Nick said and smiled.

Al-Qadir pressed a buzzer on his desk and a man entered the office. He was handed the case and he left immediately, taking the guidance system with him. Unknown to Al-Qadir, the guidance system also had a tracking device and had a fail-safe that insured that the missile would detonate.

"Acknowledged, Orion," Travis said. He then accessed the account Al-Qadir used to make payment and quickly drained it. "Transfer complete," Travis said.

Monika made her way back to the elevator, but before she got on, she pulled the fire alarm. By the time she reached the lobby, the occupants of the building were filing out of the building in an orderly fashion.

"Probably just another drill." Al-Qadir looked at Nick and picked up the phone to call security. "Is there fire in the building?"

"We haven't detected any fire; however, as a precaution we are evacuating the building. Once everybody is accounted for outside, my teams will sweep the building before we allow the occupants to re-enter, sir."

Al-Qadir hung up the phone and turned to Nick. "We should get out of the building so security can do their job."

"I understand," Nick said and followed Al-Qadir to the nearest stairwell. They exited the building and stood in the courtyard along with the other building occupants. Security made the count to insure that everybody who was in the building was out. Once the count was complete, Monika pulled up alongside Nick and Al-Qadir and pointed a plastic Glock 17 that was hidden under the seat at him. Nick grabbed him by the arm.

"I suggest that you get in the car and behave yourself."

Al-Qadir looked around at the confusion and made particular note that security had all but vanished to go in and check the building. He got in the backseat and Nick got in with him. Monika handed Nick the gun and drove toward the gate. Once they were out the gate, Monika pulled over and detonated the first of the explosives she'd set.

That one was designed to get security out of the building and move the crowd back. Once that happened, she detonated a series of cascading explosions that brought the building down. Monika rendezvoused with Jackie in the van; they rolled by the building where Xavier was waiting. They took Al-Qadir to a spot close to the US Embassy where officials of the US Army took him into custody. The team was then driven to a small, private airfield where they boarded a flight to Turkey en route back to the States.

A TALE OF THREE WOMAN

Chapter Forty-three

With business behind them, Bobby and Rain took Black to the airport. He got on the plane and told the pilot to take him to Nassau. There was one more thing that he had to do, and he wasn't looking forward to it. Jamaica met him at the airport and drove him to Paraíso.

Black went to the bar and got a drink. When he finished that, he had the bartender pour another. He was on his third Remy when Jada came in the room. She was wearing a Prabal Gurung Neoprene and Tulle Dress with sheer tulle insets and floral details that added allure to her look; and Manolo Blahnik Luxe Italian suede point-toe, four inch pumps.

Jada smiled when she saw him. Then she held up one finger and left the room. Black finished his drink and ordered another. When she came back, there was a woman with her. Since she was a bit too old to be working there, Black knew that the woman must be her mother. As she got closer, he could clearly see the resemblance between mother and daughter. Black drained the glass and took a deep breath.

"Good evening, Ms. West."

"Welcome back, Mr. Black."

Black turned to Vivian. "And this lovely lady must be your mother. I'm Mike Black, Jada's partner."

"Vivian West." Black bowed at the waist and kissed her hand. "I'm sure you don't remember me, but I met you many years ago when you used to work for André Harmon."

"You're right, that was many years ago. How long will you be on the island?"

"It is so beautiful here; I was thinking about staying."

"I am sure you'll love it," Black said and glanced at Jada. She smiled and it had the usual effect of making him want to rip her dress off her.

Vivian smiled and looked at Jada. "It was nice meeting you, Mr. Black."

"I'm sure we'll see each other again," Black said as Vivian walked away.

"Well, Mr. Black, you're back much sooner than I expected. Did you take care of your business?"

"Yes."

"That's wonderful," Jada said. She could hardly contain her excitement.

"I need to talk to you about something," Black said.

When Jada looked at him, all the excitement she was feeling was quickly drained away.

"You don't have to say a word, Mr. Black. It's written all over your face. That wife of yours has finally come to her senses."

"You're right. She has."

"I knew this was coming; I just wasn't expecting it to happen so soon. She's probably at the house right now waiting for you."

"No, she won't set foot in that house. She is at our old house in Freeport."

"Freeport?" Jada said, and it felt like somebody just stuck a knife in her and turned the blade. "Freeport, huh?"

"Yeah."

"Will I see you again?"

"We are partners; of course you'll see me again. Jada I want you to know—" Black began, and Jada put her finger over his lips.

"Please don't. I don't think I need or want to hear what you have to say next. But I want you to know that whether you like it or not, I belong to you now, Mr. Black. No other man will do. That means I am and always will be yours. Anytime you want me ... want to see me ... want to talk to me," Jada smiled, "want to have lunch with me ... I am here for you." She started to say, *Because I love you*, but thought better of it.

"A part of me belongs to you. A big part."

"I didn't need to hear that, Mr. Black."

"Sorry I said it, but I meant it."

Jada turned her back to him. He touched her on the shoulder. "I think you should leave now before I start to cry. And I don't want you to see me cry, Mr. Black. So please, just go."

Without another word passing between them, Black turned and walked away. Jada walked as fast as she could to her office. She closed the door and was able to lock it before her tears began to flow.

Black went to the docks and boarded his boat. He went below and found Oscar. "Take me to Freeport," Black said and went up on deck. He took a seat at the bow. As Oscar set sail, Black sat and thought about Jada. She was a part of him now and he wondered if he would be able to resist her.

When the boat docked in Freeport, Black caught a cab to the house that he and Shy built. "Home."

When he opened the door and went in, the first person that saw him was Michelle. "Daddy!" she screamed excitedly and ran to him. He dropped to one knee and she jumped in his arms. "I missed you, Daddy," Michelle said and kissed him over and over.

"I missed you too."

Shy came in the room carrying Easy. "We missed you too, didn't we, Easy?"

Easy smiled at his father. "Michelle, take your brother and y'all go play," Shy said. "Mommy needs to talk to Daddy."

"Come on, Easy," Michelle said, grabbing him by his hand. And they ran out of the room together.

"Hello, Cassandra."

"Hello, Michael." Black took Shy in his arms and they shared a long, passionate kiss. The feeling made her head spin. "That's the feeling I've been waiting to feel. But I guess all I had to do was allow myself to feel it."

"I've been feeling that way all along."

"I know, and I'm sorry that I took us through all those changes," Shy said, and she kissed him again.

"You don't have to apologize. I'm just glad you're home. And I'm glad to be home with you. But there is something that I need to tell you."

"I hope it ain't bad news."

"But it is," Black said as Easy ran into the room and jumped in Shy's lap.

"I tell you, Michael, your son is a lap baby. Since I've been here, this is his favorite spot. His mother must never put him down."

Black looked around to see if Michelle was coming. "More likely his grandmother than his mother. Cassandra."

"What is it, Michael? I don't like the look on your face. What's wrong?"

"His mother's dead. She was murdered two days ago," Black said, and it genuinely hurt him to say it.

"You didn't kill her, did you?"

"No. I wouldn't kill my son's mother and before you ask, I wouldn't have anybody else do it."

"I know, and I'm sorry I had to ask. I know you said you were keeping him, and I know how women are. We have a way of pushing you to do things you'd never even consider."

"No, Cassandra, I didn't kill her or have her killed."

"Are the people responsible dealt with?"

"For the most part, yes. Ms. Robinson is looking for the triggerman now. Between her and Jap, they'll find him and deal with him."

"Has she had a funeral yet?"

"No. I need to call Mrs. Collins and check on what arrangements she's made."

"Whenever it is, if you don't mind of course, I'd like to go with you. For us to go as a family."

"I wouldn't have it any other way," Black said. "Like I said, you're his mother now. I'll get our lawyer down here to get the adoption papers ready, if that's all right with you of course."

"Of course."

A few days later, the Black family including his mother, was sitting in the front row at CeeCee's funeral. For obvious reasons, it was closed casket.

After the funeral, they stayed in New York. Shy wanted to be sure that Jack was okay and Black needed an update on Monk. Then, instead of going back to Freeport, Black took the family, M included on a ten-day cruise. When they got back to New York, he took them to Europe. Neither Black nor Shy had ever been to Europe and they were both excited about the trip.

They would spend the day sightseeing as a family and then M would keep the children while Black and Shy enjoyed the nightlife. They spent a few days in London; ten days in France. The first part of the week was spent in Paris. On the weekend they traveled to Saint-Tropez, which is located on the French Riviera. From there it was off the Venice in Italy before heading to Rome. They capped off their European vacation with a trip to El Racó Beach in Costa de Valencia Spain, before going to Barcelona to catch a flight back to New York.

But Black wasn't done yet. When they got back to Freeport, Black asked M to keep the children while he took Shy to Fiji and Tahiti in the South Pacific. So Shy got exactly what she wanted. Shy wanted to be swept off her feet again by the man she loved and that's exactly what Black did. Each night she was wined and dined, pampered and spoiled. She felt loved and cared for, and protected.

Shy was happy.

ROY GLENN

THE END OF A TALE OF THREE WOMEN
THE MIKE BLACK SAGA CONTINUES IN
MISUNDERSTOOD

A TALE OF THREE WOMAN